WHEN A ROGUE FALLS
A Regency Historical Romance

ROGUES OF THE ROAD

SASHA COTTMAN

Copyright © 2021 by Sasha Cottman

All rights reserved.

No part of this book may be reproduced in any form or by any electronic or mechanical means, including information storage and retrieval systems, without written permission from the author, except for the use of brief quotations in a book review.

Chapter One

*Earl Connor's Estate
Just outside of London*

The moment Sir Stephen Moore stepped into the hallway, he sensed trouble. He grimaced at the scene which lay before him, then turned to his client. "I thought you said you had winged him?"

Earl Connor glanced in the direction of the large pool of red gore and gave a derisive sniff. "Well, he was moving a little slower than I had expected. Perhaps I got a decent shot in."

A decent shot? That amount of blood on the floor means a badly wounded man.

Stephen gritted his teeth. He hated the sight of blood, could barely stomach it.

Another night and another jealous husband. Cleaning up the private indiscretions of the *ton* was becoming tiresome. If the job didn't pay as handsomely as it did, he would walk away with no regrets.

The crimson smear on the elegant parquetry floor trailed

all the way to an open door at the end of the hall. Countess Connor's not-so-secret lover had somehow managed to drag himself away and was more than likely dying in a pool of his own lifeblood in the rear courtyard.

Just what I need.

The earl took a step forward, but the bulk of Stephen's six-and-a-half-foot frame blocked his way. He placed a firm hand on Lord Connor's shoulder and levelled him with his piercing blue eyes. "My lord, I would suggest that you let me handle this. Go back to bed and pretend that nothing happened. Or better still—attend your wife. I expect she might be in somewhat of a state of distress at having her evening so violently interrupted."

"But what if the blackguard is badly injured?"

You should have thought about that before you fired a bloody pistol at the man. Not to mention you don't seem to give a damn about Lady Connor.

Stephen took a deep breath to calm his temper. Cool heads were what these sorts of situations required. "I am a professional. Handling this mess is what you pay me to do. If your wife's friend does die, rest assured it will be somewhere far from here and your involvement will never be known. Now please, hand me the gun."

Lord Connor grumbled something foul under his breath but did as he was told. The moment the earl disappeared upstairs; Stephen headed for the door.

Outside lay a young man. Blood soaked his white linen shirt, and his breathing was labored. The fact that he happened to be the Marquess of Witham only added to Stephen's already complicated night.

"Ruddy hell," muttered Stephen. He raced down the steps and came to kneel at the stricken man's side.

"The beggar shot me," groaned Lord Witham.

"Well, you were tupping his wife, so you are not exactly in a position to complain. But fear not. I have a carriage waiting outside in the street. After I get you away from here, I shall arrange for one of London's best and most discreet physicians to attend to you."

The marquess lifted his hand. "Thank you. My papa has always said you were a decent chap."

Stephen gave a brief nod in response, grateful that for once it didn't come with the usually added words of 'unlike your father.'

All of London's elite society knew Sir Robert Moore was a devious scoundrel. Fortunately, few members of the *haute ton* were aware that his son was up to his own eyes in smuggling, kidnapping, and pretty much anything else that was lucrative and illegal.

The apple didn't fall far from the tree in the Moore family.

"Now this is going to hurt like the devil. So, on the count of three, suck in a deep breath and I will lift you to your feet. One. Two—." Stephen didn't bother with three, as he hauled the stricken aristocrat upright.

"Oh! What happened to three?" groaned Lord Witham.

"I find it is always better to let the agony flow through you," lied Stephen.

Bullet wounds do tend to sting. And hopefully, you will remember how much and do your best to avoid these sorts of situations in the future. Though I seriously doubt it.

The marquess swayed unsteadily on his feet, and for a moment Stephen feared the young lord might swoon. He tightened his hold on him. "Lord Witham, I will get you out of here, but I require a number of things from you in return."

The marquess gripped the front of Stephen's jacket and whimpered. "Anything; name it. Just get me to a doctor."

"One, keep quiet. And two, don't die on me."

It was well after dawn by the time Stephen made it back to the offices of the RR Coaching Company in Gracechurch Street. He arrived via the rear lane way, pulling his mount up near the stables.

After dismounting his horse, he handed the reins over to the company's one and only employee, Bob.

The craggy, old stable hand took one look at the blood stains on the front of Stephen's shirt and screwed up his nose. "Rough night, Sir Stephen?" he inquired.

Stephen rolled his eyes. "Bloody nobles—can't keep their tools in their trousers."

Bob had worked for the rogues of the road long enough not to ask for further details. He pointed in the direction of the main building. "His grace, the Duke of Monsale, and some other members of the company are upstairs in the office. I was instructed to ask you to join them once you arrived. Oh, and Lady Alice is also here."

Stephen glanced at his disheveled clothing. The fabric had dried but the metallic odor of the marquess's blood remained.

The sooner I am out of these clothes the better.

While bloodstained clothes weren't anything his friends hadn't seen before, Harry's wife was a different story. He was not going to greet Alice in this state.

His long legs took the stairs leading to the company offices three at a time. On the landing, he reached for the door handle then paused. He put an ear to the door. There was not a peep to be heard from within the room on the other side.

"Why is Alice here at this hour?" he whispered.

Because something is wrong.

His nerves suddenly tingled with premonition. It was rare for the RR Coaching Company directors to meet this early in the morning. Monsale, for one, never rose before the hour of ten. Not unless there was a crisis.

And they are all here, including Alice.

Taking a deep breath, Stephen took a firm hold of the

handle and pushed open the door. The vision which met his gaze set his pulse racing.

Lord Harry Steele, Lady Alice Steele, The Honorable George Hawkins, and the Duke of Monsale were assembled around the weather-beaten, grand table, which took up much of the main room. Heads turned in his direction as he stepped through the door.

True to form, his fellow rogues of the road furnished him with their customary stony faces, but when he looked at Alice, a shiver of dread slid down his back.

Her eyes were teary, and her face flushed. The tremulous smile she offered to him, a portent of doom.

Definitely bad news. Bloody hell.

Stephen gave a quick bow. "Lady Alice. Please excuse my state. I wasn't expecting to find anyone here at this hour. Give me a minute to change, and I will be with you all shortly." He took a step toward the hallway and his room.

Monsale nodded. "Of course, take your time, my friend."

Stephen stopped dead in his tracks.

What the devil? Monsale never speaks to me like that, never uses that tone.

He spun on his heel and faced the gathering.

All the company members were present this morning. All except Augustus Trajan Jones. Gus had sailed to France two days earlier, and if all had gone to plan, he should be on his way back to England onboard his yacht the *Night Wind,* a cargo of contraband brandy safely hidden below the weather deck.

Stephen looked from Monsale to Harry and then to George. "Gus?" he managed in a voice barely above a whisper.

The mere thought of the smuggler's ship sinking somewhere in the English Channel or heaven forbid him having been captured by the customs militia filled Stephen with fear.

Gus. Sweet lord, please no.

What would he do if this was the news?

Lord Harry rose from his chair and came to Stephen's side. He placed one hand on his shoulder, the other held out a folded and sealed letter. "I am so truly sorry, Stephen. It's your father. His lawyer delivered this to my house an hour ago. Apparently, it was the only address they had for you."

Stephen's shoulders sagged with relief. Gus was alive and well. He took the note, then without a second glance tossed it onto the table. His father could wait.

"I will make myself presentable first, then read it. A few minutes won't change the fact that the black-hearted devil is dead."

He pretended not to hear Alice's gasp of surprise. Of course, she was shocked by his reaction to the news of his father's passing. Alice Steele came from a real family—one where the members actually gave a damn about one another. Stephen couldn't remember a time when his sire had ever shared an ounce of affection with him.

And that's because it never happened.

In his room, he shrugged out of his jacket and bloodied shirt, letting them drop on the floor. He would bundle them up later and get Bob to take them to the local washerwoman in nearby Pudding Lane. She knew exactly what to do with those kinds of stains. And also, how to keep her mouth shut.

From his battered travel trunk, he retrieved a fresh, clean shirt. The act of dressing occupied his mind, keeping it from tempting thoughts of regret. Stephen was a master when it came to avoiding unwelcome emotions.

With his attire now set to rights, he checked himself in the mirror. A flannel and some water from a pitcher removed the remaining traces of last night's dirty work from his face and hands. The Marquess of Witham would live and hopefully had learned a painful lesson from his near-death experience. Hopefully.

He closed the door of his room and calmly walked back

along the hallway. Stepping into the main office space once more, he gave his assembled friends a wan smile.

Let's get this over and done with.

He retrieved the lawyer's letter and slipping his thumb under the wax seal, broke it open. A quick read confirmed the news. His father, Sir Robert Moore, was indeed no longer among the living.

There were a few other pertinent details regarding balances held on deposit with various financial institutions and mention of the title deeds to the family home in Witley, but other than that, there were no actual details about how his sire had died.

No surprise there.

"I'm so terribly sorry," said Alice. The heavily pregnant wife of his fellow rogue of the road came to Stephen, arms open wide, offering comfort. He reluctantly accepted her attempted hug.

It was odd to be receiving any form of consolation over the death of a man he barely knew. A man he would not grieve.

When a tearful Alice finally released him from her attentions, Stephen turned to the other men. "Did my father's solicitor say anything else?"

Monsale sighed. "Apparently, he got into a fight with someone a week ago and a knife was produced. In the ensuing brawl, your father was stabbed. He died at Moore Manor the day before yesterday."

And no one thought to send word to me because they assumed, I wouldn't bother to make the trip all the way to Surrey.

Stephen wasn't completely sure what he would have done if someone had arrived on the doorstep of the RR Coaching Company during the past week and announced that his father was at death's door.

Probably sent them away with a flea in their ear.

Alice took a hold of Stephen's hand and gave it a reassuring pat. "When was the last time you saw your father? I hope it was a moment that you are now able to treasure."

His mind was suddenly filled with the memory. It hadn't been pleasant then, and the pain of it still burned even now. "I haven't seen my father in six years. I spied him across a crowded card table at Whites club. When I raised my glass of brandy in salute to him, he didn't even bother to acknowledge me," replied Stephen.

Harry came to his wife's side. "I'm sorry, my dear, but not all families are as close as yours or even mine for that matter. Sir Robert was never one for his relatives."

For the first time since he had received the news of his father's death, a pang of longing and regret pierced the fortress wall which surrounded Stephen's heart.

Explaining his parents to other people had always been a great source of humiliation for him. His mother had abandoned him not long after birth. After she had returned to her family in Scotland, she refused pointedly to ever have anything to do with him.

His father had been little better. He had housed, fed, and paid for his son's education, but that had been the extent of things. Familial relationships were not part of the Moore family way of life.

"Alice, thank you for your kind thoughts. I really do appreciate them. It is sad that my father is dead, but even sadder to know he wouldn't give a damn if I cried over him or not." Tears pricked at Stephen's eyes, and he hurriedly blinked them back.

His gaze drifted over Alice's head and landed on Monsale. His friend gave a brief nod. If anyone in the room could understand how he was feeling right now, it was the Duke of Monsale. Only Andrew McNeal could best Stephen when it came to having a cold, detached, and dead father.

"Well, I suppose it means a trip down to Witley is in order to claim the body and arrange a decent burial," said Stephen.

His father's timing couldn't have been worse. Stephen had plenty of other pressing matters to deal with in London. Important things.

"Would you like us to come? I expect having some friends standing alongside you at the graveside would be nice," offered George.

Stephen considered George's kind proposal for the briefest of moments, then shook his head. "Thank you, but I wouldn't want to waste your time. The grave service will be short and without fanfare. Considering how Sir Robert lived his life, I don't anticipate having to deal with a crowd of weeping mourners."

As soon as the funeral arrangements could be made, he would bury his sire, check with the steward of his father's estate to ensure that everything was in order, then make his way back to London. There was no point in him lingering at the house.

In time, he would sell the place and leave with no regrets. It had long ago lost any promise of ever feeling like home to him.

As Harry put his arm around his wife, and they moved away, Stephen caught the baffled look on Alice's face. Of course, she couldn't understand how he felt. His lack of grief was so foreign to her view of the world. A person had to have held something and known it was theirs in order to experience the pain of loss. For Stephen, that hadn't ever been the case.

How can you mourn for something you've never had?

Chapter Two

"Why does having to heat a house cost so much?" muttered Lady Bridget Dyson. She was sure that every time she saw a new bill from the coal merchant, the price had gone up. At least her late husband, Rupert, god rest his soul, had left her with enough of an annual income to meet these sorts of expenses.

For once, he did something right by me.

She set the invoice aside and turned to gaze out the sitting-room window. The Dyson house, number 12 Berkeley Square, sat just past the corner of Bruton Street, facing onto the lush green of the square. On days like this, when she considered what had become of her life, Bridget liked to imagine she was a young girl once more, perched high up in the branches of one of the imposing plane trees. A happy child without a care in the world.

"Instead, I am working my way through dull household accounts."

Yes, but you are venturing back into society this evening. And you are planning on wearing that gorgeous silver and gold silk gown.

It was odd to be thinking of colors once more. But she had

done her time in donning the drab black of a widow, making certain she respected the memory of Rupert. She had been most scrupulous in observing society's expectations as to her manner of dress and conduct. In her time of mourning, she had been careful not to put a foot wrong.

The fact that she and Rupert's marriage had been an utter disaster was neither here nor there. Appearances were what counted.

Rupert had been dead for a year; her sentence as his wife and grieving widow was now over. It was Bridget's time to move on—to begin to shape and rebuild her life into one of her own choosing and maybe even find happiness.

A tall fair-haired gentleman passed by on the opposite side of the street. Bridget leaned closer to get a better look.

Well-dressed. I like the cut of his coat. I wonder if he likes to dance.

Stepping back into society was something she was looking forward to; it would make a welcome change from the mind-numbing quiet of her recent existence.

Perhaps I could take a lover. I am a widow. It is quite acceptable.

She smiled at the thought. Polite society was always prepared to turn a blind eye to those sorts of liaisons as long as they were conducted discretely.

And thanks to Rupert spreading a spiteful rumor about her, Bridget's reputation as the *Barren Baroness* would no doubt guarantee that there would be plenty of gentlemen willing to share her bed. A young, unattached woman able to indulge in a sexual relationship without the risk of pregnancy would be perfect in the eyes of many a man.

A rap on the sitting room door roused Bridget from her musings. Her attention shifted from the window to her brother, Tristan, as he marched into the room.

"Hello. I wasn't expecting you," she said.

And you were not announced. I must have a word with the butler.

She rose, moving out from behind the desk. Her normally cheerful sibling wore an expression of dark worry. But before she had a chance to ask what was wrong, Tristan had spun on his heel and headed back to the door.

He closed it firmly behind him and turned the key in the lock. "My apologies for the sudden visit. As you and I were meant to be going to the opera tonight, I hadn't planned on coming over this morning, but something has come up. Something which cannot wait."

Dread suddenly gripped her. "Is it Papa?"

Earl Linton had not been a well man for a number of years. Bridget had fully expected to bury her father long before she had to say farewell to her strapping and fit husband. But she had learned that life had a strange way of turning out, of throwing up unexpected and unwelcome surprises.

Tristan shook his head. "No. It's Mama."

Mama?

"She has been at it again."

Bridget winced, knowing exactly what *it* meant. The countess loved to play card games; cribbage was her favorite. She was an expert at the game and loved to win.

While many members of the *ton* went to private parties to socialize and dance, Lady Linton only attended if there were tables at which she could play and gamble.

She was also a cheat.

"I thought she'd promised she wouldn't do it anymore. Not after the ugly fallout I had to deal with following the Duchess of Bedford's midwinter ball," replied Bridget.

"Yes, well, old habits appear to die hard," said Tristan.

She had still been in mourning at the time, so Bridget had fortunately been spared having to witness the embarrassing sight of two lifelong friends exchanging harsh words through the open windows of their respective carriages.

The last thing Bridget needed as she stood on the cusp of

reentering society was to yet again be having to smooth over the wounded pride of another of her mother's friends.

"Who is it this time?" she asked.

"I'm not sure. I received a letter early yesterday. It was signed only with an initial," replied Tristan.

He dipped his hand into his coat pocket and withdrew a piece of paper before handing it to Bridget. She unfolded it, her heart sinking as she took in the cold, hard words.

Lady Linton,
On several occasions of late, you have been seen miscounting your hand while playing at the cribbage tables. While the odd arithmetical error can be excused, your ongoing inability to correctly announce your score cannot, however, be tolerated.
It is time to pay for your sins.
You have until the end of the month to hand over the sum of 2,000 guineas or the full details of your dishonest ways will be printed in every newspaper in London.
In the meantime, you will place an advertisement in The Times *noting your acknowledgement of this letter, after which you will receive further instructions.*
You should, of course, keep this matter private. If not, I will make my accusations public.
Lady Linton, the choice is yours—your husband's purse or the ruin of your family.
N.

Bridget quietly folded the letter and handed it back to Tristan. For a moment, she feared she might faint. "Who the devil is 'N?'"

"Believe me when I say I lay awake all last night racking

my brains as to who it could be, but I have no idea. I expect 'N' is just a nom de plume."

Two thousand guineas. And I was worried about the cost of heating.

Tristan took a hold of Bridget's hand. "I know it is only ten o'clock in the morning, but I would kill for a brandy."

Her gaze went to the nearby sideboard. One of Rupert's bottles of expensive French brandy sat unopened on the top. Imbibing at this hour was not the proper thing in polite society, but then again, Bridget doubted that Fordyce's *Sermons to Young Women* had a passage on how one should conduct oneself upon receiving a blackmail letter.

Tristan released his hold on her, and Bridget went to fetch him a drink.

She had just poured him a generous glass, when he cleared his throat. "You might want to pour yourself one too. Mama is waiting outside the door. She wanted me to tell you first before you saw her. That is why your butler did not announce our arrival."

"Oh," Bridget sighed.

She could understand Tristan's way of thinking. A stiff drink might well be the lesser of two evils. The other being to go and seize her mother by the shoulders and try to shake some sense into her.

Bridget's hand was trembling as she set down the bottle of brandy. No, she wouldn't succumb to either temptation. "Have your drink. I will fetch Mama." Bridget unlocked the door and flung it open.

Any notions of yelling at her mother vanished as soon as her gaze settled on the countess. Lady Linton's tear-streaked face and reddened eyes melted Bridget's heart in an instant.

"I have been so very naughty again. I'm sorry, darling," whispered Lady Linton. The countess rushed past her and into the room.

Gritting her teeth, Bridget followed, closing the door behind them.

Tristan managed to set his glass aside just in time as Lady Linton threw herself into his arms.

"Alright, we know you are sorry. Calm down, Mama. You promised no more tears." While he held their mother in his comforting embrace, Tristan's gaze met Bridget's.

"What are we going to do?" she asked.

Tristan prized his mother off him and helped her over to one of the plush, well-padded sofas. The countess took up a spot at one end, her head resting in her hand.

Bridget averted her gaze as she recalled the endless hours she too had spent seated in that same spot while crying her eyes out over the cruel behavior of her late husband.

But this situation with her mother was different to the many occasions she had found herself in as a result of the actions of a cruel spouse—different in one very important respect. With Rupert, the tears had been shed in despair and hopelessness. At least with the blackmailer, they had an ounce of hope.

If worse comes to worst, we shall just have to pay the money.

"I've a plan to deal with this blackguard who is trying to ruin our family, but it is not going to be an easy task," announced Tristan.

The countess began to sob once more, this time loudly.

Bridget did her best to maintain a composed and calm veneer. Having two tearful women wouldn't aid their cause.

"Mama and I are leaving for Linton in the morning. We can't have her going home and facing Papa on her own. I fear it will end in disaster."

She caught the anger which simmered in her brother's words. He would be the one who had to undertake the ghastly task of informing their frail father that his wife had put their family reputation on the line. It didn't bear mentioning that if news of Lady Linton's repeated indiscretions ever became public, the Linton name would be damaged beyond repair.

While Lady Linton continued with her tears of self-pity, Bridget did her best to dampen her own smoldering rage. "Mama created this problem. She should be the one to have to deal with it, not you." Her gaze fell on the slumped form of her mother, and to her dismay, Bridget found herself wishing ill of one of her parents.

I am so angry with you right this minute. I don't think I can muster up a kind word.

Tristan sighed. "I'm afraid I might be getting the better end of the bargain. It is you who has the hardest task ahead of them. While I am doing my best to keep both our mother and father from falling apart, it is you, sister dearest, who will have to deal with the matter of the blackmailer."

She went to protest, but Tristan shook his head.

"We have to keep this quiet. And I must protect our family. Papa most of all. I have no desire to become Earl Linton anytime soon. If the blackmail money needs to be paid, I will return to London and deal with our bankers."

Tristan dug his hand into his coat pocket once more and retrieved a card. He handed it to Bridget.

Discretion assured. Results guaranteed.

"What's this?" she asked.

Tristan stepped closer. His gaze darted to their mother then back to Bridget. He leaned in and spoke in a low voice. "That is the card of the man who is hopefully going to solve our problems."

Bridget turned the card over. There was not a name or address anywhere to be seen. Just four words of promise. "Who is he?"

"You will find out soon enough when you meet him. He has asked that the use of his name be kept to an absolute minimum." Tristan pulled his watch from out of his vest pocket and flipped it open. "And in answer to your next question—in about an hour's time. I've given him your name and address. I have also paid his initial fee."

Turning it over and over between her fingers, Bridget pondered what sort of man would be behind such a nebulous calling card. On one hand he proclaimed his skills and record of success, while on the other he remained nameless. "Alright. I will meet with this mystery man. But if I think he is a charlatan set only on getting money out of us, I warn you, I won't hesitate to unmask him. Who is to say he is not behind the scheme to blackmail us; have you considered that?"

The card folded in Bridget's grasp as Tristan settled a hand over hers. "He comes well recommended by some close friends of mine. People with titles and power. People whom I trust."

The countess stirred from the sofa, and getting to her feet, slowly walked over to join her two children. She wore a sheepish expression on her face, one which had Bridget frowning. "I haven't told either of you this before now, but I have used this gentleman's services in the past."

"What?!" exclaimed Tristan.

Lady Linton straightened her spine and met her son's gaze. "The fact that none of you ever found out about either of those occasions only goes to show how good this man is."

Bridget took a hasty step back as her brother seized their mother by the arm and dragged her toward the door. "I think it is time we left. I feel a most urgent need for a heart-to-heart with our dear mother. Bridget, send word if you want anything from me. We are off home to pack. I'm not waiting for tomorrow; the family coach will be leaving London today."

The door rattled in its frame for several seconds after Tristan slammed it shut behind him.

Bridget examined the crushed calling card one more time, then headed back to the sideboard. After opening a bottle of whisky, she filled a glass with more than she should, downing it all in one go.

Her future and that of her family stood on a knife's edge. If the Lintons could escape from this nightmare without it becoming public knowledge, she might finally have a chance to find contentment. To put the misery and heartache of her past to rest. She had as much invested in the outcome of the next few weeks as anyone else.

"Whoever you are, I will do all that you ask to save my mother's reputation. But if you are a scoundrel seeking to profit from our misfortune, rest assured I will do everything in my power to destroy you."

One person had already ruined her life. She would not stand for it to happen a second time.

Chapter Three

Later that morning, Stephen stood staring out the window of Lady Bridget's drawing room watching the passing parade of London life. After the vexing night he had experienced, followed by the news of his father's death, it was a pleasant relief to undertake such a mindless activity.

He turned as the door opened and through it stepped a tall, blonde woman in a gray gown. She held out a hand in greeting. Stephen took it and bowed his head.

"I am sorry if I kept you waiting. My household staff can be unreliable at times, and I was only just informed of your arrival," she said.

"That's perfectly alright. I was a little late for our appointment. This morning has not run according to my expected schedule." One couldn't plan for the news of a parent's death, let alone when it had been the result of a violent altercation. Not that his new client needed to know any of those sordid and rather sad details.

"Lady Bridget Dyson, pleased to meet you," she said.

"Sir Stephen Moore."

A look of understanding and possible recognition

appeared on her face, along with the hint of a blush on her cheeks.

"We have never met, Sir Stephen, but I am a friend of Lady Naomi Steele, and she has made mention of you at times. I must confess that I have heard the odd rumor about her brother, Lord Harry, so I am not entirely surprised to discover that the man Tristan has hired to help us also happens to be one of Harry's business colleagues."

He fixed his customary light air to his demeanor and smiled at her.

Everyone in London thinks they have the measure of the RR Coaching Company. Trust me, Lady Bridget, you only know what we allow you to perceive as being the truth.

"As far as I am aware, Lord Harry is a respectable businessman. My work with him is restricted to that of the RR Coaching Company. I cannot speak to anything else that he may be involved with, other than to advise you not to listen to speculation and rumor."

It wasn't a lie. She wasn't to know that the RR Coaching Company was a front for all the illegal dealings of the rogues of the road.

Bridget nodded. "My apologies if I have offended you in any way."

His gaze drifted from the drab of her gown to her face. A pair of almost iridescent blue eyes stared back at him, and his heart skipped a beat.

How did I miss those stunning eyes?

Stephen's mind slipped back into the days of his youth. Lady Bridget's eyes were almost a perfect match for the warm waters of Lake Annecy in France. *Utter perfection.* A man could gladly lose himself in those blue pools.

Goodness gracious she is a delight. Gosh.

When had he started speaking like the queen?

Get a hold of yourself, man. You are not one for getting into a wobble over a woman. She is your client. Calm down.

He blinked hard in an effort to regain control.

"No offense taken, Lady Dyson. If I am honest about it, I think Lord Harry enjoys creating rumors. A man who dresses as outrageously as my good friend does, knows full well that people are inclined to talk about him."

Bridget smiled. "Yes. While I haven't been about in society much over the past year, one cannot ever forget the spectacle of Lord Harry Steele making his entrance to a party clad in a bright purple and yellow banyan with matching fez. The stuffed peacock he carried under his arm was quite the talking point of the evening."

Stephen chuckled. "You haven't seen him getting about with Milton, his piglet. Now that is a sight. Even the piglet seems to think it amusing."

He wasn't going to make mention of the fact that he too had a soft spot for Milton, or that rubbing the piglet's belly and hearing its little grunts was a source of particular enjoyment for him.

A moment of awkward silence followed before Bridget motioned to the nearby sofa. "Shall we get started? I expect your time is valuable, Sir Stephen."

He took the seat on the sofa that Bridget offered, setting his leather satchel on the occasional table to his left. He lifted the table and placed it in front of him, then carefully opened the satchel.

It was a moment of well-crafted theater, all designed to convey a sense of purpose and comfort. "I have some preliminary notes with me, which I thought we could go over this morning. I've also made arrangements for a small, discrete notice to be placed in the newspaper confirming receipt of 'N's letter."

He liked to open his first meeting with a new client in a strong fashion. By appearing to have sat up all night considering their particular problem, he found it helped to win them over, to gain their trust. And considering that many of the assignments he dealt with were of a delicate nature, having a calm patron was always a plus.

Bridget took the seat opposite him. She pointed at the papers. "When did my brother speak to you? I was only informed of my mother's indiscretion earlier this morning."

Hello. We have a perceptive one here. I shall have to tread carefully with her.

It would appear that Lady Bridget Dyson had a mind to match her bright eyes. Stephen appreciated intelligent women. "The viscount and I spoke briefly late yesterday morning. I would have come to see you earlier today, but an unexpected, private matter arose overnight, which required me to make some arrangements."

It was ironic that Sir Robert Moore, who having never spared much time for his son during his life, was now making demands on Stephen in death. He resented such obligations coming from a man who clearly hadn't given a damn about him.

Bridget rested her hands in her lap and sighed. "I am not sure what my brother has told you, but this is a serious matter. So please tell me if you are unable to give it your full attention. If that is the case, then I shall seek the services of someone else."

He lifted his gaze from the papers and met hers. From his years of service as an agent of the crown; and now his career in the murky underworld, Stephen had developed the ability to comfortably hold his nerve against others. Bridget quickly looked away. She was worried.

Of course, she is. Her mother is a card cheat, and their family stands on the edge of social ruin. Go easy on her. You are not the only one having a trying day.

"As I explained to your brother, I am more than capable of dealing with blackmailers. In fact, it is a bit of a specialty of mine. Rest assured, I will place all my energies into solving this problem."

Her fingers threaded tightly together. His words had clearly not yet won her over.

And then she fixed Stephen with a cold, hard stare.

She doesn't trust me in the least.

"I understand that my mother has utilized your services in the past. And yet here we are, paying you once more to deal with a blackmailer. It speaks to me that this is more than just a touch coincidental."

Damn. Damn. Damn.

Stephen didn't like clients talking about him behind his back. When he had dealt with Lady Linton's earlier problems, he had made her sign a non-disclosure agreement. By confiding in her children, she had breached their contract.

He wasn't going to touch on the subject of Lady Dyson's thinly veiled accusation of him seeking to line his pockets from her family's misery. Or even perhaps being the cause of it. She wasn't the first, nor likely the last client to come to that erroneous conclusion.

He shuffled the papers and picked up a copy of his standard four-page contract. He handed it to Bridget. Tristan Linton had already signed it, but since Bridget was now going to be his principal client, it was important to get her mark on it as well. "I need you to sign this before we go any further. The work which I undertake in dealing with these situations can at times drift into somewhat gray areas of legality. While I protect my clients, I also expect them to play their part. That includes keeping our discussions a secret."

Lady Linton had not been a problem for him in the past. He was determined that none of the Linton family were going to become one now.

Bridget set the document on the table and crossed her arms. "What if I refuse to sign the contract? What happens then?"

She thinks that she is testing me. All she is doing is playing into the hands of the blackmailer.

Frustrated, Stephen snatched up the contract, gathered the rest of his papers, and stuffed them into his satchel. He quickly closed it. "Nothing happens. Good day to you, Lady Dyson. I won't waste any more of your time, and I ask the same of you."

He got to his feet and gave a curt bow.

He is annoyed. Good.

Tristan would be livid if he knew what she had said to the man he had tasked with helping their family, but trust wasn't something Bridget held in great supply. Years of being poorly treated and blamed for not having provided her husband with children had left her deeply suspicious of others and their motives.

If Sir Stephen took offense at her words, then in her reckoning, it was a good thing. It meant that he took his job seriously. The last thing Bridget needed was a self-important rogue making a mess of things. She wanted a man who could take charge and get results. Someone who could deal with a dirty blackmailer.

Results guaranteed.

Bridget shifted quickly from her place on the sofa, stepping in front of Stephen as he moved clear of the table. She bounced off him, staggering a step back as he failed to check his stride in time. "Oh," she exclaimed.

He was a large man. Tall, broad shouldered, and not an ounce of fat on him if his well-toned thighs were any indication. A mountain of infuriated male stared down at her. "Lady Dyson, please let me pass."

But she was not done. Taking a determined step forward, Bridget set both hands to the front of Stephen's black jacket. Mustering all her resolve, she lifted her head and looked up at him.

Dark blue eyes, almost sapphire in their depth, held her captive. There was an obvious touch of displeasure about his countenance, but she sensed he wasn't by nature unkind. He wouldn't be the sort of man to hurt a woman because he felt like it—because he could.

"What color would you say your eyes were, Sir Stephen? I don't think I have ever met anyone with such entrancing peepers before."

The hard edge disappeared from his visage, replaced by an easy grin. A low rumble rose from his chest and a rough laugh echoed in the room. Whatever she had said, he clearly found it amusing.

"Peepers. What grown woman uses that word? Did you just escape the nursery; and are in need of your nanny?"

Bridget's cheeks burned. He was right. It had been a silly thing to say. "I'm sorry. You have me at sixes and sevens. Is that the usual effect you have on women, Sir Stephen?"

He bent, and their noses were mere inches apart. "Believe me, Lady Dyson, when it comes to women, I have found I can make them feel or do pretty much anything I command."

Her heated cheeks were not the only part of her body suddenly flushed with warmth.

And I bet you have them all begging for more.

"Would you like me to sign the contract?" she asked.

He blinked slowly, and Bridget held her breath. In a flash, he produced the papers and handed them to her.

"I thought you would see things my way."

She took the contract and hurriedly signed it, after which, to Bridget's relief, they resumed their seats.

Thank god he didn't leave.

"Now, Lady Dyson," he said.

"Bridget. Please. I promise you I don't have an affinity with my married title. If I were able, I would go back to my maiden name of Linton. Unfortunately, my late husband stipulated that I must keep his name if I wished to remain in this house."

"You could always remarry."

Bridget shook her head. A second marriage would never be in her plans. Once had been bad enough. She had learned her lesson. "I should think that a man such as yourself would have heard the rumors about me. Rupert did make a concerted effort to ensure that as many people as possible knew that I was incapable of carrying a child. That makes me somewhat of a less than attractive prospect for any gentleman seeking a wife. Not fit for purpose."

There, I said it. Now we don't have to bother with skirting around the subject.

Stephen reached into his satchel and took out a small notebook. "People are the worst when they are intent on causing pain. I did know your husband, and it would not be disingenuous of me to say that I didn't care for him or his opinions."

A spark of hope finally lit in Bridget's heart. It was comforting to know that Sir Stephen Moore didn't hold Rupert in any sort of high regard. It spoke to her of a man with at least a modicum of decency.

"Back to the problem at hand. This blackguard who is trying to extort money from your family. I have given some thought as to whom 'N' might be, and my initial suspicions are that this person is someone known to your mother. From my previous dealings with Lady Linton, I am aware that she keeps a diary. I sent word earlier to your brother that he should have it delivered here. Has he sent it?"

Bridget rose and hurried over to the bookcase. She had wondered why her mother's diary and notebook had arrived earlier, now she understood. "I trust you will treat anything you happen to find within these pages with the utmost discretion. Did you also want her notebook?"

"No, just the diary. She seems to keep a good list of names and dates in it."

Her heart was racing as she handed Stephen the diary. All her mother's lies and secrets were likely contained in that pale-blue book.

"Believe me, Bridget, I know so many dark things about London society that your mother could have perpetrated all the crimes of Emperor Caligula, and she still wouldn't hold a candle to what some of our so called 'betters' have done."

Resuming her seat, Bridget didn't meet Stephen's gaze. She had fought against her inbuilt prejudices, and now found herself wanting nothing more than to trust this man.

Please be the man I think you are, as I am badly in need of a knight in shining armor.

Chapter Four

With the promise to Bridget that he would spend the next couple of days going through her mother's diary looking for clues as to the possible identity of 'N', Stephen set out later that day for Witley. He overnighted at the whitewashed public house *The Running Mare* before arriving at his father's Surrey estate early the following afternoon.

As he rode up the long, dusty drive, a sudden thought took him. This wasn't his father's estate any longer.

It's mine.

Pulling on the reins of his horse, Stephen slowed his mount to a walk. The same giant oak trees of his childhood still lined either side of the road leading to the main house. The low stone walls marked out the boundaries of the nearby fields.

The place didn't appear to be much different from what he remembered, but the fact that he was having to rely on old, faded memories rather than recent ones pained him. It had been many years since last he was here.

This was his family home, yet it had never felt like it.

Term breaks spent with his friends and their families

during his school days had shown him the truth of what had always been missing in his life. A loving mother and father.

"When are you ever going to stop grieving for something that was never yours? You can't mourn the loss of a dream," he muttered.

Some people were fortunate with relatives, others not. He just happened to be one of the latter.

He dug his heels in and urged his horse on. He wanted to spend the least amount of time here. To know the circumstances of his father's death, hold a brief funeral service, and then get back to London.

Lady Bridget Dyson, the comely widow was counting on him.

I am keen to see her again.

Thoughts of running his fingers through the gentle curls of her long, pale hair quickly sent his mind to wicked places. To what an afternoon spent with the luscious blue-eyed Bridget could be like. Of setting his lips to her naked flesh.

Steady on.

A quick shake of the head had Stephen pushing that ridiculous notion away. Bridget Dyson was a client, nothing more. Though if he were honest, she was the most fetching client he had ever dealt with; but nevertheless, her family were still paying for his services.

Mister Granville, his father's long-serving steward was waiting for him when Stephen made his way out of the stables and toward the manor house. There were quite a few more gray hairs and lines on his face since last, they had met, but Granville still had a sprightly manner about him. "Sir Stephen, it is good to see you. Though the circumstances could have been better."

Stephen nodded. "Yes."

There was no point in either of them making an attempt at flowery words of condolence. Having been a fixture at Moore Manor all of Stephen's life, Granville had borne witness to the distance which had always existed between father and son. Firstly, by father, then as the years passed, by son.

"So, what happened?" asked Stephen.

Granville motioned toward the house. "Would you like to come inside, and we can discuss this in private?"

Stephen hated the house. It's sandy-colored ashlar stone walls held nothing for him but cold, empty memories. "I would much rather we walk."

At the end of the yard was a solid, wooden gate. Stephen opened it and stepped onto the lush green grass of the small high field which abutted the grounds of the house. In the distance more verdant pastures stretched out before his gaze. This was prime grazing land.

His father might have failed as a husband and a father, but he had chosen well when it came to be selecting someone to manage the Moore estate. Granville had excelled in his role.

A few yards inside the paddock, Stephen stopped and turned to Granville. "Well?"

The steward cleared his throat. "Your father hadn't been spending much time here of late. Just the odd quick visit. When he suddenly arrived last week, it was obvious he was not well. He fell from his horse in the stable yard. We managed to get him inside, and that's when we discovered his injuries."

Stephen scowled. "Did he say where he sustained the knife wound? His lawyer mentioned an altercation of some sort. Was he stabbed in London or in a nearby town?"

If it had been somewhere close by, his father's attempts to reach the estate would make sense.

"Apparently, it was outside of London. He didn't say much of what had happened, other than he had got into a fight with another gentleman. It took him two days to get here, but he said he was determined to make it," replied Granville.

Why come all the way here to die? What possible reason could he have had to return to Moore Manor when he was so badly wounded?

"I eventually convinced him to allow me to summon a doctor to come from Guildford, but by the time he arrived, it was too late. Your father passed away during the night."

Stephen sighed. He could add 'who had killed his father' to the long list of queries he had been building since a child. Not that it mattered anymore. He was never going to get a single one of them answered, including the most pressing. The question which would forever haunt him.

I am your son, so why have you always hated me? As I can see, my only crime against you was being born.

"Where is my father now?"

"In the crypt at All Saints church. The vicar is pressing for us to get the burial service underway as soon as possible."

Delaying the inevitable wasn't going to do anyone any good. And Stephen wanted to leave for town first thing in the morning. The quicker he was away from this place, the better.

"Alright. Get whoever wants to come to the service assembled, and I shall meet you at the church in an hour," replied Stephen.

"Very good, Sir Stephen. Shall I make a time for you and me to discuss estate matters and the transition of ownership?" replied Granville.

The old man is really dead. This place is now mine, but I just can't think about it right now.

"Perhaps we should wait until I can find a moment to give things my full attention."

Granville's cheeks turned a scarlet red. "I humbly beg your pardon. That was most uncivilized of me. Of course, you wish to spend some time in quiet reflection of your father. I would never wish to impose on your hour of grief."

Even the trusty old family steward seemed to expect Stephen to feel *something* over the loss of his father. Why society suddenly decided that all manner of customs and social dictates should come into play just because someone had died was beyond him.

I don't feel anything.

Stephen wouldn't be shedding any tears, nor wasting hours in silent regret. He had given up on that long ago, coming to the firm conclusion that none of it was worth his emotional energy.

It was time to set Granville straight on the sort of funeral Sir Robert Moore was going to get, as well as the amount of time his son intended to invest in mourning him.

"Let's get the service done and my father buried. After which, I shall walk across the road into the *White Hart* and shout everyone there a whisky to toast the passing of Sir Robert. After that, I will return here, pack some papers, and make ready to head back to London at first light."

His hand was on the gate before Granville finally mustered a reply. "I thought, perhaps . . . of course. Very good, Sir Stephen."

Stephen's long strides took him quickly back past the stables, toward the long drive. He wasn't even going to bother with his horse.

Granville's kind words had rattled him.

What he needed was a long walk, alone. Time away from people to check that the locks on his heart were secure—that emotions of any kind had not managed to find their way in.

Because if there was one thing Sir Stephen Moore was certain he wouldn't ever do, it was to waste a single tear for a man who had never once called him son.

Chapter Five

By the time he reached the church, Stephen had his emotional armor firmly back in place. It was impenetrable—nothing would get through. Of that he was determined.

At the crunch of boots on gravel, he turned. The sight which greeted his gaze instantly melted his iron breastplate.

"Oh no. Oh damn," he muttered.

A small cart appeared in the courtyard of All Saints. On board were Mister and Mrs. Granville, the latter dabbing at her eyes with a handkerchief. Behind them slowly walked the estate staff and what had to be at least half the residents of the village of Witley. All come to pay their respects to the late Sir Robert.

How am I to deal with this?

He gritted his teeth, praying that no one would come near him and offer their sincere condolences. But when he saw the downcast eyes and sad expressions on their faces, it was clear he was in for a trying time.

Hold your nerve and get through it. That's all you have to do.

While the rest of the mourners headed to the graveside and gathered around it, Stephen waited for his steward. If he kept the Granvilles close, using them as a shield of sorts, then the locals might not be tempted to come and talk to him.

He could only hope.

The small cart drew to a halt, and Mister Granville stepped down. He helped his wife alight, then turned and helped a third person. Stephen looked closer. He hadn't realized there was anyone else in the cart.

It was a young boy. From the look of him, Stephen guessed he was about five or six years in age. He could very well be one of the Granville's grandchildren, but from the masterful cut of his jacket and the quality of his boots, it was obvious whoever his parents were, they had money.

Mister Granville took the boy by the hand and led him over to Stephen.

"I gathered as many people as I could at such short notice. If you wish me to delay the service a little longer, I am sure the parish priest won't mind."

"No. Let us have this done with," replied Stephen.

His words were addressed to his steward, but his gaze remained fixed on the boy.

The young lad was digging up the dirt with the toe of his boot and fidgeting in the way that all small children do when they don't want to be where they are; when they would much rather be free to run around and play.

"Come now, Master Toby, you promised to be on your best behavior this afternoon. Make your introductions to Sir Stephen," said Granville.

The boy huffed. He let go of the steward's hand and placed an arm across his stomach. He bent at the waist and bowed. "Sir Stephen, my name is Toby. I am honored to make your acquaintance."

Stephen was still taking in the pale brown of Toby's hair when the boy righted himself and met his gaze. Blue eyes the exact same shade as Stephen's stared back at him.

It was as if someone had punched him hard in the gut,

such was the shock of recognition. Of seeing someone who could have easily passed as himself at that same age.

He slowly blinked, doing everything in his power not to look at either Mister or Mrs. Granville.

Who is this boy?

Stephen remained rooted to the spot. He didn't notice when Granville reached out and took hold of Toby's hand once more. It was only when Mrs. Granville stepped past and touched her fingers gently on Stephen's arm, that he finally stirred.

With hands clasped tightly behind his back, jaw set hard, Stephen pivoted on his heel and followed in their wake.

§

The burial service itself was brief. The local vicar gave a short but eloquent speech about Sir Robert. Of the employment the estate had provided to the local villagers over the years. He made special mention of how well the manor house had been maintained and the church's gratitude for the recent funds Sir Robert had donated to help repair the roof of the vicarage.

Granville nervously cleared his throat, and Stephen stifled a snort.

I bet the old man had no idea that he had given the church that money. Tight old bastard that he was, he would have refused if Granville had actually asked.

When the vicar made mention of the new lord and master of Moore Manor, Stephen suddenly found his boots to be of great interest. He was sure that his hard-as-stone heart had formed tiny cracks at the edges. He didn't want to look at the locals, to see their sad and pity-filled faces.

He especially didn't want to look at the young boy, Toby. To think what his existence might mean.

It was only when the last of the mourners shuffled their way toward the church gate and the tavern across the road that Stephen finally let out the breath he was certain he had been holding for the better part of an hour.

But when he caught sight of Granville standing alongside Toby watching as the dirt was thrown over Sir Robert's coffin, Stephen finally decided it was time. He moved forward.

"So, Master Toby. Where is it that you live?" he asked.

The boy looked away uncertainly, then straightened his shoulders. Someone had been teaching him how to address his betters when they spoke to him. "Sir Stephen, I live in the big house. Mrs. Granville looks after me," replied Toby.

"And what about your mama?" he asked.

He was treading carefully, doing his utmost not to spook the boy. If Stephen's growing suspicions were proven correct, then he and Toby would have a lifelong connection.

"Mama is in the churchyard." Toby pointed to a headstone a few yards away. He turned his head and buried it in the folds of Mister Granville's coat.

"And what about your father?"

The boy gave a half shrug.

Oh, bloody hell. His mother is dead, and he doesn't know who his father is or was.

His father had always claimed to be meticulous when it came to making certain not to leave any by-blows, but the boy standing in front of Stephen was clear evidence that sometime in the not-too-distant past, Sir Robert had slipped up.

I have a brother.

Chapter Six

In the end, Stephen shouted several rounds at the *White Hart*, his need for a stiff drink greater than his desire to be alone. By the time he walked back to Moore Manor, he was comfortably numb. After a spot of supper, he retired to bed.

At the top of the stairs, he paused. His old room was to the left, and if he had any respect left for his father, he would have gone and slept in there. Sir Robert was barely in the ground, and the transfer of ownership to Stephen was yet to be finalized.

"Sod it," he muttered.

As far as he was concerned, Moore Manor was his to do with as he pleased. The rest was mere legal formalities.

Tonight, he was going to sleep in the master bedroom.

Opening the door to a room he had never been permitted inside before today was a strange experience. For a moment, he wondered if he would sense his father's presence. That Sir Robert's long ownership would have somehow left a mark.

His gaze took in the simple dark blue coverlet and the matching curtains. There was a plain beige woolen rug on the floor. Unlike the rest of the house, where gilded paintings hung on almost every wall and in the case of the grand dining room, antlers, and boar heads prevailed, the master bedroom was completely devoid of adornment.

There was no sign of this room belonging to anyone from the Moore family.

This room could exist in a hundred different homes, and you wouldn't ever pick that it was from here.

His father had always been a man of style and fastidious taste, yet the master bedroom of his family home was so plain that it bordered on austere.

"And yet again, Father, you reveal yourself to be a man who I never knew."

Stephen shrugged out of his jacket and quickly rid himself of the rest of his clothes. From his satchel he retrieved a cheroot and lit it with a taper from the fire.

Someone thought to light it. Perhaps Granville read my mind.

Sleeping naked at home had only been a recent development for him. During his time as an agent for the British crown, he had always slept fully clothed, a pistol by his side. Even now when accompanying Gus on his yacht to Europe, he only ever removed his boots.

But tonight, he would indulge.

He pulled up a chair and took a seat by the fire. When his bare ass touched the soft fabric of the chair, he grinned. There was something deliciously wicked about lounging around in the buff.

During his tenure as Lord Harry Steele's house guest, his host had complained whenever he found Stephen sitting naked in the drawing room at Grosvenor Street. Even society peacocks seemed to have their limits when it came to them returning home from a night of drinking and carousing only to stumble across their friends relaxing in their birthday suits.

But with Harry now married and Stephen living out of a small room at the RR Coaching Company offices, his opportunities for lazing about in the nude had of late been few. In the privacy of the master bedroom at Moore Manor, he was going to relish every moment of it.

As he settled in to enjoy his smoke, Stephen pondered the future. Moore Manor was too far from London for him to be able to use it as a permanent base. Like his father before him, this would be a place purely for the occasional visit. Its main purpose was to serve as a means to provide him with an ongoing income. To supplement his earnings from his other career.

And hopefully in time, allow him to do as Harry had done and step away from a life of shady dealings.

The land was fertile, able to support a good head of Southdown sheep whose wool had always fetched a good price with the merchants in Yorkshire.

Granville can handle the estate. Though I might look to close up the house and save some blunt. A small cottage in the village might be more to him and his wife's taste.

In time, if he managed to cobble together enough money, he might be able to either buy or rent a nice place in town. Somewhere he could invite his friends to come and visit. And after they had all gone home, he would be at his leisure to smoke and drink in naked peace. A perfect plan.

Resting his head against the chair, he closed his eyes. The long, testing day had finally caught up with him. Sleep beckoned.

He opened his eyes long enough to flick the half-smoked cheroot into the fire before settling back to snooze.

Tomorrow he would be on the road to London and back to the fetching Lady Bridget Dyson.

She strikes me as the sort who might be in for a spot of naked lounging by the fire. Or perhaps she could be tempted into something more. Now there is an idea.

Stephen fell into a deep sleep. He dreamt of a naked, fair-haired woman, her legs either side of his hips as she rode him in front of a warm, blazing hearth. She wore a sultry smile as their bodies sought mutual sexual satisfaction.

He couldn't wait to see Bridget again.

Chapter Seven

When morning came, Stephen was up, dressed, and ready to leave well before eight o'clock. If he kept up a good pace, he could make it most of the way back to London today. An early start the following day, and he wouldn't have wasted the best part of a week in travelling to the far-flung outreaches of Witley, Surrey.

He didn't bother with breakfast. The sooner he was on the road, the quicker Moore Manor would be behind him. His day was well planned, and it was his to do with as he saw fit. He was the master of his own destiny.

After a cursory glance around the downstairs area, which failed to produce either Mister or Mrs. Granville, he found a piece of paper and left them a short note. With his satchel tucked under his arm, Stephen stepped out into the yard, his destination, the stables.

The stable boy was holding the reins of Stephen's saddled horse, which pleased him greatly. The rest of the scene, however, had a frown set quickly to his face.

In the yard, Mister and Mrs. Granville were standing either side of Toby. His brother. Mrs. Granville had a small travel bag in her hand. Stephen took one look at the bag and figured it wouldn't take a genius to guess its contents.

As he approached, Mister Granville came forward. "Before you go anywhere, Sir Stephen, may I have a word?"

There was a definite *I'm not taking no for an answer* edge to the steward's voice. At the same time, Mrs. Granville straightened her back and glared at Stephen. These people meant business.

"Something tells me I don't have a lot of choice," grumbled Stephen.

He and Mister Granville moved to a distant corner of the yard, well out of earshot of anyone else. The moment they stopped and faced one another; the old man started in on him. "I know what you are going to say. That the boy is not your responsibility. That your father was a terrible parent, and if you take Toby on, there is every chance that you will transpire to be the same. You had no idea Toby even existed until yesterday, and you can hardly be expected to take on the role of his guardian."

The list seemed endless.

Stephen desperately wracked his brains, seeking another good reason as to why he should leave the boy at Moore Manor and forget about him. Attempting to deny any familial link with Toby seemed at best petulant. He wasn't that cruel. The boy was obviously Sir Robert's byblow.

"I don't have time for a child. I am a busy man," replied Stephen.

It's the truth. What am I to do with him while I am out on a job? I can't possibly take him to France or Spain with me.

Mister Granville growled. The glint of a man wellprepared for battle shone in his eyes. Stephen didn't want to know how long the steward had been practicing his speech. It was far too eloquent and well-thought-out for his liking.

"There are such things as nannies and housekeepers. You

could engage one, Sir Stephen. Toby needs you, and dare I say . . . you need him," said Granville.

Stephen gave a derisive snort.

That's preposterous. I don't need anyone. Let alone a child. That's why I don't ever intend to marry or have a family.

He was in a tight bind, but he was prepared to negotiate. Everyone had a price.

"I will pay for the boy's upkeep and education. You and Mrs. Granville both seem perfectly capable of taking care of him. I can even look to increase your annual wage if that sweetens the deal."

Granville stepped forward and smacked his hand against the front of Stephen's jacket. "Sweetens the deal? This is your brother we are talking about, Sir Stephen, not a bloody horse you are seeking to trade," he snapped.

He swore at me! Who the devil does he think he is?

Stephen raked his fingers through his hair and sighed. Clearly there was no point in trying to argue with the man. He had to quickly find a resolution that saw them meeting somewhere in the middle. He couldn't afford to cave.

Then he had an idea.

"How is this for a compromise? I go back to London today and seek to make preparations for Toby's eventual relocation. Over the next few months, I shall make inquiries as to a child's nurse for him, along with a suitable school."

Mister Granville slowly shook his head. "I know the lad's existence has come as somewhat of a shock."

"That's an understatement if I ever heard one," replied Stephen.

All five feet four of the steward stared him down, which considering the height difference between them was quite a feat. "But you are Toby's only living relative. His mother and father are both dead. If you abandon him, he will be all alone in the world."

Granville may not have meant to, but those words

instantly shamed Stephen. And for a man who had spent many years living on the edge of the law, he was not accustomed to feeling anything like that emotion. Life was hard, and a man involved in his line of work couldn't afford to be weak. Or to have much in the way of scruples.

"I'm not abandoning him. He will have a roof over his head and three hot meals a day. It's more than many other bastards ever get." He pushed past Granville and made straight for his horse. A brief nod was all he could manage in the direction of Mrs. Granville and Toby.

Taking hold of the reins and placing one foot in the stirrups, Stephen swung up and settled himself into the saddle. He glanced over toward Mister Granville.

"I will send word once I have selected a school."

With the horse's head turned toward the front gate, he dug in his heels. The horse leapt away. If Mister Granville called anything out to him in reply, Stephen didn't hear it. He didn't want to have anything to do with raising a child.

He made it as far as the end of the drive before he pulled on the reins and brought his racing steed to a halt. Head bowed, he wrestled with his guilty conscience.

"Oh, bloody bollocks," he muttered.

He tossed the reins aside as he jumped down from the horse. His mount wandered away to nibble on some grass, leaving Stephen to grapple with his dilemma all on his own.

Granville's words had struck deep, right to painful memories long buried. He had thought himself strong enough to withstand the steward's pleas, but the look on Toby's face as he passed him by had almost brought Stephen undone. He knew that look only too well; it was one he had also often worn as a young child.

It was the look of hope.

Before he realized what he was doing, Stephen was kicking up a stone with the toe of his boot. Just like the boy had done at the church. Nervous habits appeared to run in the Moore family blood.

My blood. My family. He is my family.

He had grown up without siblings or any real presence of his parents in his life. Toby was destined to walk the same lonely road that Stephen had done during his younger years.

"And look how that has turned out for you."

Emotionally repressed. Cold and at times heartless, he was the creation of parental disinterest.

And if he left now, abandoned Toby when he needed him the most, all he would achieve would be to create his brother in his own image. He wasn't sure of a lot of things, but of one he was certain—the world did not need another broken Moore.

"What am I going to do?"

It wouldn't be easy, raising a boy on his own. He didn't have a wife or female relatives to support him. But he did have friends.

I can give him the material things in life. He will never want. Perhaps if I can speak to Alice, she might be able to help.

Lady Alice Steele was warm-hearted and kind. She wouldn't be the sort to turn her back on a young boy, especially not when he was in need of a mother. A friendly smile and the odd hug were all he would ask of her. It was more than he had ever received.

It's better than nothing.

He wiped away the tears which had sprung up from nowhere. How many times had he walked this long, lonely drive from house to road weeping as a child? Too bloody many.

"If this all ends in a mess, at least no one can say I didn't try."

His horse lifted its head as Stephen approached and gave a friendly whinny in greeting.

Yes, I know. I am doing the right thing. Or at least I hope I am.

Five minutes later, with Toby seated in front of him and the boy's things stuffed into his saddlebags, Sir Stephen Moore galloped out the front gate of Moore Manor.

He had just become a parent.

Chapter Eight

Going out in society was the last thing on Bridget's list of enjoyable activities right at this very minute. Instead of mixing with London's elite, all she wanted to do was to crawl under the bed clothes and hide.

But that would mean admitting defeat. And accepting that the person who was trying to blackmail her family had already won.

She had endured enough of those days while married to Rupert. Had heard so many of the spiteful whispers about her being the *Barren Baroness* to have developed somewhat of a steel spine. If she hadn't, she would have taken to her bed long ago and stayed there.

Stepping alone into the party at the Duke of Redditch's elegant mansion in Grosvenor Street that evening, Bridget sensed every eye was fixed on her.

You are a widow taking her place back in society. That is the only reason why people are interested in you, nothing more.

"Bridget! I am so glad you came." The tall figure of Lady Naomi Steele appeared through a gap in the gathering.

Bridget sighed with relief.

Thank heavens for understanding and loyal friends.

Naomi and Bridget had known one another for many years. She had cried in the arms of the Duke of Redditch's daughter too many times to count. Apart from her mother, Naomi was the only other person who truly understood the depth of misery that Bridget had endured during her marriage.

"I had to come. We agreed it was time for me to rejoin society, so here I am." The quiver in Bridget's voice betrayed her.

Before she could protest, Naomi had taken her by the arm and was leading her out of the foyer and toward the stairs. Naomi gave a wave to the duchess as they headed up to the second floor. "Just helping fix Lady Bridget's hair, Mama. We won't be but a moment."

They had barely made it inside Naomi's bedroom before the door was closed and locked. Naomi, God love her, didn't go in for a comforting hug. Bridget wasn't sure if she would be able to maintain her composure if her friend did.

"What is going on? I've seen that look on your face and heard that miserable tone in your voice all too many times in the past. It can't be that blackguard Rupert because I have been to the cemetery on more than one occasion just to make certain he was dead," huffed Naomi.

Bridget smiled through her tears. Everyone should have a fierce friend like Lady Naomi Steele.

"It's Mama. These are tears of frustration and rage because of her. She's been cheating at cribbage again, and this time someone has called her out on it. They are demanding money."

"Oh, no. Oh, Bridget, I am so sorry."

Naomi knew all of Bridget's darkest secrets, while she in turn kept Naomi's ongoing heartache over the Duke of Monsale in her safe care. "She promised she would stop. But the temptation was apparently too much."

Naomi pursed her lips. "What are you going to do about it?"

Bridget hesitated, unsure as to how much she should reveal about Sir Stephen Moore's involvement.

You did sign that contract, and with it comes the non-disclosure clause.

She knew Stephen to be a friend of Naomi's brother, Lord Harry, but she wasn't sure if Naomi knew exactly the line of work in which Stephen dealt. This moment called for a degree of discretion. "My brother has engaged someone to assist with the problem. Tristan and Mama have gone off to the country for a short time, leaving me to deal with the gentleman. I understand him to be quite experienced at handling these sorts of matters."

A sly grin appeared on Naomi's lips. "If Tristan is as clever as I think he is, then I know exactly who your brother has hired. You can say his name."

Bridget hesitated before speaking. "Sir Stephen Moore."

Naomi's grin spread into a wide smile. "That is good news. If anyone can hunt down the villain who is seeking to harm your family, it is Stephen. Do you know when he will be back in London?"

His absence from the city was news to Bridget. When he said he had some personal matters to attend to, she had assumed he would still be in town. This was a worrying development.

"I wasn't aware that he had left London. Are you sure he is reliable?"

The last thing she needed was someone who flittered off to the country and only got around to dealing with her pressing problem when they felt like it. She had thought Stephen to be trustworthy, now doubt crept back in.

I have less than a month to get this settled or my family's reputation is shot.

"Stephen is a thorough professional. All of my brother's

friends who are engaged in such special assignments always treat them with the utmost seriousness. He only left town because he had to bury his father," said Naomi.

Oh. I was so rude to him. And I pressed him as to the need to get on with dealing with my problem. How heartless must I seem?

"I had no idea. I will apologize the next time we meet."

Naomi dropped onto the edge of her bed, spreading her arms out wide. She patted the silk coverlet. "Come and sit with me. Mama and Papa won't instruct the staff to call anyone into the dining room for at least another hour. My parents prefer to mingle with their guests before forcing everyone to the formality of the dining table."

Bridget did as she was told, taking up a spot on the gold-and-silver-striped bed covering. Guilt over the way she had spoken to Stephen simmered in her mind.

The poor man. He must have been beside himself with grief. Any wonder he wanted to leave when I questioned him.

"Did you know Sir Stephen's father?" she asked. It seemed the polite thing to do to inquire about the man.

Naomi shook her head. "Not really. He didn't have time for people like us. Us being anyone who was important in his son's life. Sir Robert Moore was what my father would politely call a bit of a rake. My brother, Harry, has used some *very* choice words about Stephen's father over the years."

"What do you mean?"

"Sir Robert was more interested in bedding other men's wives than he was in being any sort of father to Stephen. And don't ask me about his mother. She apparently disappeared back to Scotland not long after his birth. He was basically discarded by both his parents."

The *ton* had its fair share of unhappy marriages, but few people actually abandoned their spouses and children. It must have been a terrible union for Lady Moore to have done such a thing. No woman would willingly give up her child without good cause.

And to think, all I have ever wanted is a child of my own.

"What about Sir Stephen? Is he cut from the same cloth as his sire?" He had captured her interest at their first meeting. If things went smoothly with solving her blackmail problem, perhaps Stephen might be someone she could become friends with or possibly something more.

Her fingers bunched up the fabric under her hand.

"Bridget are you thinking what I think you might be about Stephen?" replied Naomi.

The heat burning on her cheeks was all the reply Bridget needed. When she lifted her head and met Naomi's gaze, her face felt ready to burst into flames. "You said I needed to get back on the horse. If Stephen is someone who loves and leaves women, then why not? I wouldn't be risking my heart over him."

She had no plans to ever marry again. In his will Rupert had left Bridget the use of the house for the rest of her life. There was nothing to stop her taking on a lover, and when she tired of him, finding another.

Naomi leaned in and smiled. "Well, he is a giant of a man, and I suspect that is in all manner of things. So, if you are planning on riding Sir Stephen, just make sure you hold on tight."

A laughing Bridget buried her burning face in her hands.

I have to do something to help Naomi and Monsale finally get together. This girl is badly in need of a lusty husband and a marital bed. And she would make an excellent duchess.

"He has also openly stated that he never intends to marry, so you and he might be a perfect match," added Naomi.

Bridget stilled. Stephen was a devilishly handsome specimen of the male species. And if he was indeed a rake, they could both approach a discreet liaison without any expectations.

Hurry back to London, Sir Stephen.

Chapter Nine

A *few days later*

After dropping Toby off at Harry and Alice's house that morning, Stephen made his way over to see Lady Bridget Dyson. The clock was ticking on the blackmailer's demands.

Any fears of his about asking Alice to help with his new ward had been quickly swept aside the minute she and Toby met. The youngster and the heavily pregnant Lady Alice had taken to one another in an instant. From the moment he opened his eyes in the morning, it was clear that Toby was concerned with one thing only, and that was getting over to number 16 Grosvenor Street.

Stephen suspected that a great deal of the appeal was due to Harry and Alice's piglet, Milton, running around the house. He hadn't the heart to explain to the boy that Milton wasn't a pet, but rather the eleventh of his name in a long line of breeding pigs raised by Harry for the Duchy of Redditch.

If Stephen had been honest about it, he was feeling just a

tad jealous. Even Harry appeared to have established himself higher in Toby's world than his big brother.

Yes, well he doesn't know you are his brother. As far as he is concerned, you are just the man who took him from the only home he has ever known and made him come and live in a couple of rooms of a coaching company.

Once this job with Lady Bridget was done and dusted, he had to do something about sorting out a proper home for Toby and himself.

He was still making plans to engage the services of an agent to find a suitable house when the front door of Bridget's home opened, and the butler ushered him inside.

Stephen followed the man into the drawing room where he and Bridget had first met. Bridget rose from the sofa as Stephen was announced. "Thank you, Taylor. That will be all."

He was halfway through a bow when she hurried over and took a hold of his hand.

"I am so, so sorry," she said.

Stephen scowled, taken aback by her behavior. This was the same woman who had given him a hard time when they had previously met.

An embarrassed smile sat on her face. "Lady Naomi Steele told me about your father. I am sorry for your loss and also for the disgraceful way I behaved when you were here last week."

I forgot she was a friend of Harry's sister. I shall have to mind my words.

"That's perfectly alright, Lady Bridget. You were not to know. While I wasn't particularly close to my father, his death still came as a bit of a shock. I was not quite myself that morning, but rest assured you have my full attention today."

Awkward exchanges over, they both took a seat.

"Oh, and this came from the blackmailer while you were away." Bridget handed him a note.

He gave it a quick perusal then set it aside. Apart from repeating his demands, the scoundrel hadn't added anything further. "That is good," he said.

"Why is that good?"

He pointed to the letter. "It means he is still thinking about how to proceed. A hardened professional would have had the whole thing planned out well in advance. Which indicates to me that we are dealing with either a first-time blackmailer or a rank amateur."

His money was on it being the former. Someone had read too many books and got the idea of communicating via the newspaper from one of them.

"So, you are hoping it means he will make a mistake?" asked Bridget.

He gave her an appreciative smile. She was a smart woman, thinking about the problem beyond just handing over money.

"While I was away, I took the opportunity to go through your mother's diary."

Stephen withdrew Lady Linton's diary from his satchel, along with a piece of folded paper and placed them on the table.

After settling Toby to sleep in his room at the RR Coaching Company offices, he had stayed up late last night and read the diary. Most of the entries in the book were fortunately mundane and held little of note. But slowly a list of possible suspects had begun to take shape. By the time he finished thumbing through the pages, Stephen had eight names which had sparked his interest. Eight people who he had decided were worthy of further investigation.

Harry's mother was unfortunately one of them. While he would dearly love to strike the Duchess of Redditch off the list immediately, Stephen was a professional, so no stone could be left unturned.

He pointed to the piece of paper. "Can we talk about these

people? Some of them you might think are beyond reproach, while others may give you reason enough for thought. We must, however, consider all possibilities."

Bridget picked up the note and examined it. She sighed. "Every one of these people are my mother's nearest and dearest friends. She will be utterly crushed if it is any of them."

Stephen silently nodded. Friends betraying friends was the currency of the *ton*. Lives and fortunes were lost over petty jealousies and silent vengeance. "Please don't take this the wrong way, but your mother has an unfortunate habit of burning her friends. The previous work I have undertaken for her has involved people whom she has known for many years. None of them are currently on the list, but I will still make subtle inquiries as to the state of their current relationships with Lady Linton."

In his line of work, it wasn't unknown for people to harbor grudges long after things had supposedly been smoothed over.

"Yes, well they do say that revenge is a dish best served cold. I wouldn't be surprised if the blackmailer did transpire to be someone that Mama would never have suspected."

§

"I can't believe any of these people would seek to hurt Mama or my family," said Bridget.

The first two people on the list were her godparents. Her father already owed them money; it wouldn't do any good for them to ruin the Linton family. She was sorely tempted to pick up the pencil and run a line through the names. But Stephen's words about it being someone close to Lady Linton kept rolling around in her head.

Her gaze settled on the next name. "The Duchess of Redditch, really? You can't be serious?"

Stephen frowned at her. "Everyone needs to have their alibis and motives checked and scrutinized. No one, even Kitty Steele, comes off the list without my say so. You have engaged me to do a job, and while your assistance is most welcome, you must allow me to succeed by whatever means I deem necessary."

Bridget held back a sharp retort. She didn't appreciate being spoken to in such a manner. Stephen might be in charge of the case, but that didn't mean she was prepared to bend completely to his will. Rupert's war against her had cost Bridget much of her self-regard; she was not going to yield up what little dignity she had managed to regain over the past year. If it meant standing up to Stephen, then so be it. It was her family's money and future at stake.

But within reason. Remember why he is here. This is about more than your bruised pride.

"Alright. Now let us discuss the next person on the list," she said.

It was late in the afternoon by the time they finally finished going through the life history of the other five people mentioned in her mother's diary. Stephen didn't just ask about their recent interactions with Lady Linton, he went back years. He was nothing if not thorough.

Bridget was exhausted and hungry. Stephen, meanwhile, kept writing more of his copious notes.

When the clock on the mantel chimed the hour of five, he paused and raised his head. "Is that the time? I had no idea. We will need to finish up for today. I have to pick young Toby up from Harry and Alice's house. If he has been running around as much as he usually does, he will be in need of an early bed."

Who is Toby?

"Is Toby your son? I didn't realize you had children."

I thought he was an avowed, lifelong bachelor. He doesn't behave much like a parent.

He met her gaze. "Toby is part of the estate I recently inherited from my father. Until a few days ago, I had no idea he existed."

He sees a child as goods and chattels? How sad.

Whoever Toby was, and whatever his connection to Stephen, at least he was being cared for; many other men would simply have ignored the boy or shipped him off to a far-flung place. Out of sight, out of mind.

Stephen gathered his papers and stuffed them into his bag. "There are still a significant number of questions regarding your mother's friends which need answering. I don't think we are going to find much more in the pages of the diary, so may I suggest we undertake some reconnaissance work together?"

"Oh, and how are we to do that?"

He slowly looked her up and down. Bridget shivered as his gaze roamed over her body, stopping and then lingering on the swell of her breasts. An appreciative grin formed on his lips. "We should go out into society together. I am more than happy to accompany you to a select number of events. Places where we can observe the suspects on the list. You are out of mourning, aren't you?"

Impertinent scoundrel.

"Yes, but what about you? Your father has only just died."

He dismissed her concerns with a lazy wave of his hand.

I would love to slap that hand of yours.

"The rules are not the same for men. As a widow, society expects you to observe a formal period of mourning. And considering that the last time I saw my father he made a point of giving me the cut in public, I can't see anyone taking offense at my not wearing a black armband in his memory. I haven't even bothered with a death notice in *The Times*."

Bridget flinched at the callous remark. She may not have loved Rupert by the end of their marriage, but she had been determined to do everything correctly in order to honor his memory. There was no point in trying to fight the double standard which applied when it came to women. A year of wearing black and remaining out of society was expected.

"We shall attend some of the private parties and gatherings that your mother normally does. I need to know who else is a regular attendee of them, and who will seek us out. It will help firm up the list of suspects," said Stephen.

Bridget blinked as realization suddenly dawned on her. "You think the blackmailer will have the effrontery to talk to us? By Jove that's bold!"

Stephen got to his feet. "In my experience, blackmailers are odd creatures. They take perverse delight in watching the discomfort of their victims. If your mother and brother are not in town, I would bet a thousand guineas that the scoundrel who is targeting your family will find it impossible to resist making your acquaintance."

"Really? I don't think I am that interesting, but if you think it will help," she replied.

He held out his hand and an intrigued Bridget was unable to resist offering hers. He raised her hand to his lips and placed soft, warm kisses on the fingertips.

The heat of his breath had her swallowing deeply.

"Believe me, Bridget, you are quite the captivating female. We might be spending time together as part of the case, but I assure you, I find every moment in your company delightful. I can't honestly say I can think of anything I would rather do than spend an evening with you. Who knows where it might lead?"

With you sharing the night in my bed.

The pulse of desire thrummed through her body. The touch of his hand on hers promised all manner of unspoken wicked delights. Of what he might offer to do to her with those long, thick fingers.

It had been an eternity since a man had caressed her in the

way a woman desired. Needs and wants that had lain dormant for the longest time now stirred to life.

Their gazes met, and she offered him a tremulous smile. He returned the favor with a sly grin which set heat pooling in her loins.

You handsome rogue, I am not the only one having lustful thoughts.

"I am ready to do whatever you ask," she said.

"I shall hold you to your words, Bridget."

She silently prayed that was not all he planned to hold against her.

Chapter Ten

At first, Stephen thought the noise was a stray animal, perhaps a cat mewling. But as he stirred from sleep, his ears caught the words mixed in with the pitiful sound.

"Mama. I can't find it."

After climbing from his bed, he stumbled through the dark hallway, banging his shoulder hard against the door frame as he entered Toby's room.

Damn.

Rubbing his arm, he peered into the dimly lit space. The light which shone through the window revealed a small figure seated upright in the bed against the far wall.

"Toby, what's wrong?"

"I can't find my rattle," sobbed the boy.

Stephen shook his head. What was a young lad doing still having a rattle with him when he slept?

"Do you really need the rattle?" There was a sense of pleading in his voice. If Toby did need the damn thing, where was he going to find a rattle at this ungodly hour?

"I always hold it when I can't sleep. Mama gave it to me."

Oh, great. It's not just any old rattle.

"When did you have it last?" replied Stephen.

I don't recall a rattle in his things. Please don't let it still be at Moore Manor.

"Mrs. Granville promised that she had packed it."

Lighting a candle, Stephen quickly retrieved Toby's small bag. He pulled out a few items of clothing. There weren't many. The next thing his fingers touched was a small wooden handle. As he lifted it out of the bag, a gentle tinkle echoed in the room.

"You found it!" exclaimed Toby.

Thank god.

"Here, tuck it under your blankets, so you don't lose it," said Stephen, handing it over.

Toby clutched the rattle tightly in his hands. He snuggled back under the covers, and Stephen came and perched on the edge of the bed. He brushed a hand over the boy's face, wiping away the last of his tears. "You have your rattle. Now, try to get some sleep."

He made to move off the bed, but a small hand settled over his. "Will you stay with me until I fall asleep? I am frightened of this place."

Stephen's cold heart stirred at the long-buried memory of being a small boy and feeling all alone in the world. Having a roof over one's head and a full belly wasn't the same as knowing you were protected.

Or wanted.

"Alright. Close your eyes, and I promise to stay here until you fall asleep." Stephen shifted to the end of the bed and rested his head against the wall.

I can't believe I am playing at parent, but anything for peace and quiet.

꧁

When the following morning came, Lord Harry Steele ambled up the stairs of the RR Coaching Company and, finding no one about, peeked in through the open door of Toby's room. On the bed, Stephen lay beside Toby, the small boy wrapped up safely in his arms. Toby's rattle rested between them. They were both sound asleep.

A knowing grin found its way to Harry's lips.

He is starting to understand what being a parent is all about. Alice will be pleased.

Chapter Eleven

That evening, Bridget stood studying her reflection in the cheval mirror of her dressing room. Her figure hadn't changed at all over the years. Other women may have considered that a blessing, but to her, it was a sign of failure. Her inability to provide Rupert with a son had eventually torn their marriage apart. And then he had become cruel.

There was a slight hint of crow's feet at the corners of her eyes, but that was to be expected. Time never stood still.

"Not exactly how I expected to be making my formal reentry into polite society," she whispered.

Instead of appearing on Tristan's arm at the opera and then doing her best to retreat quietly into the background, she was going to a party with Sir Stephen Moore while on the hunt to unmask a blackmailer.

She had chosen a dark green silk gown for the occasion. It was the closest thing she had to black. Respectable widows made their reentry into society with slow, measured steps, knowing that each one would be noted and judged.

A rap at the door saw her maid enter the room. "Lady Bridget, Sir Stephen Moore has arrived and is waiting in the foyer."

Bridget nodded. "Please tell him I shall be down shortly."

Alone again, she turned back to the mirror, grateful that her calm exterior did not betray her feelings of apprehension. What if they didn't succeed in finding the person who was trying to destroy her family? Or worse still, if they did and the blackmailer felt threatened enough that they made good on their promise to take their accusations against Lady Linton public.

I must trust Stephen. This is not the first time he has dealt with such a situation.

After picking up her evening shawl from a nearby chair, Bridget took a deep breath and steadied her nerves. Fearful or not, she was going to do everything she could to defend her family.

There was movement on the staircase, and Stephen glanced up. The vision of loveliness which met his gaze had him staring in wonder.

Lady Bridget Dyson was a rare creature. She stirred strange emotions within him, ones he couldn't quite discern. There was lust, obviously. A man would have to be half-dead not to react to such a beautiful woman. But there was definitely something else.

What is it that you do to me?

He shook himself from his musings as Bridget reached the ground floor. Stepping forward, he dipped into a low bow. "Lady Bridget. You look absolutely divine."

A smiling Bridget met his gaze as he righted himself. "I was about to say the same thing of you, Sir Stephen. I honestly don't think I know a single man in all the *ton* who can do justice to an evening jacket the same way you do."

He chuckled. "The skills of a good tailor. It is all in the cut of the cloth. Underneath all this, I am actually four feet three and slight of figure."

When Bridget laughed at his jest, Stephen's heart swelled. He hadn't been lying when he told her he was looking forward to spending time in her company. Tonight, had been on his mind all day.

She took his offered arm, and they walked toward the door. Bridget leaned in and whispered, "Someday you will have to show me what is under your jacket."

Not while you are still a client. But if we can unmask the blackmailer, who knows. I am sorely tempted.

He could offer her a private liaison, but nothing more. Unlike Harry, he wouldn't do anything rash like falling for his client. Or heaven forbid—marry her.

A short, passionate affair could be just what the enticing widow needed to set her back into society. And Stephen was more than willing to be the man for the job.

Chapter Twelve

Heads turned as they walked into the private party in a house in Silver Street a short time later. Bridget quickly realized that most of the attention was not on account of her but rather Stephen. The rustle of fans being opened and fluttered in his direction, while their owners outright ignored her, bordered on rude.

Am I invisible?

She tightened her hold on his arm in an obvious statement of claim. Stephen might not be hers, but she was paying for his time. They had arrived together, so that should at least afford her some sort of acknowledgment or respect.

He glanced down at where she held him in a vice-like grip. "If you grasp my arm any harder, I might lose all feeling in it. Rest assured, Bridget, you have my full and complete attention this evening."

Why did he have to notice?

"I don't know what you are talking about. I am simply nervous at being out in polite society once more. It has been a long time."

A deep, dirty laugh rumbled in Stephen's chest. The temptation to pinch him was strong, but she had an inkling he might like it.

"Come. Let us get a drink, and then we can mingle and observe. As soon as the ladies realize that you and me, for want of a better word, are a couple, they will look for another distraction. And you will be able to mercifully withdraw your claws from my flesh."

Only if you offer to sink your teeth into my skin.

Imagining what Stephen would look like fully naked sent a ripple of heat coursing through Bridget. Her tongue swept over her lips at the prospect of his manhood being on display for her private appreciation.

He is a big man. I have no doubt that he is sizable in every way.

She couldn't muster the willpower to stop picturing Stephen in all his glory. How magnificent it would be, and just as important, how skilled he would be with it?

She put a hand to her cheek. "Is it me or is it hot in here?"

He gave her a sly side eye. "It's you. And I have a sneaking suspicion I know exactly what you are thinking. Naughty girl."

She stumbled, and Stephen quickly reached out, stopping her from taking a tumble. His large hands, resting on her waist, he set Bridget standing steady on her feet once more.

For a moment, she simply stared at the floor, too embarrassed to meet his gaze. When she finally did lift her head, he gifted her with a soft smile. Mischief glittered in his eyes. "Relax, Bridget. I was only teasing. Now how about we go and get that drink, and you forget what anyone else here, apart from me, is thinking about you."

"I'm sorry."

"Don't be. You are by far and away the most captivating woman in the entire room. And I am hoping that since every eye is on us, you will be the honey we need in order to lure our villain from his lair."

Well, that was rather clumsily put, you are a clod. I think you even managed to mix your metaphors. Bees and honey. Spiders and lairs.

If Bridget wasn't a bundle of nerves already, Stephen was convinced he had just made certain of it. He had meant to reassure Bridget that she was both a stunning woman and also a vital part of the plan to unmask the blackmailer, but it hadn't quite come out that way. Now she was probably thinking he only wanted her for her looks, not her intelligence.

You are a dolt of the first degree.

Pushing aside thoughts of his ham-fisted attempt to placate Bridget, Stephen forced himself to concentrate on the task at hand, observing other guests. They were here for a reason.

They made their way into the ballroom, and Stephen immediately spotted a problem. There were four large round tables in the center of the grand room taking up the space where, during a ball, people would normally be dancing. Every available seat was occupied.

Around the outside were other small gatherings of seated party guests, some in conversation, the majority watching the card games.

Damn. How are we supposed to be inconspicuous in this place?

The setup wasn't exactly conducive for slyly observing the goings-on of the evening. Wherever they stood, they would be seen. He was a tall man, hard to miss. If there was one thing Stephen was never comfortable in being, it was conspicuous when he was trying to blend in.

He led Bridget away from the tables and with his back turned to the gathering, faced her. "This is not good. I foolishly assumed that there would be an orchestra and dancing. The card tables are normally set to one side and the people moving in and out of the games can be observed from a discreet distance. I very much doubt that if our blackmailer is here tonight, they are going to risk attempting to make contact with you."

"We can't up and leave. We've only just arrived," she replied.

She had a point. The evening's hosts might not take too kindly to be seeing recently arrived guests suddenly turning tail and heading out the door. They may consider it rude and a personal slight. With Bridget attempting to make her way back into elegant society, they had to be circumspect in their behavior for her sake.

"Why don't we take a seat and watch a couple of games? I have spotted one of the people on your list here tonight. Seeing how Lady Bell is going with her cards might give us an idea as to whether she may have reason to try to get money from my family," said Bridget.

It wasn't ideal, but at least the evening wouldn't be a total waste.

"Alright," he replied.

Drinks in hand, they managed to find a couple of chairs, and they took up a spot not far from the table where Lady Bell was playing.

An hour later, and Stephen was completely engrossed in a game of cribbage. With the first set, he had barely had time to get a handle on the *tells* of the various players before it was over, but by midpoint in the second game, he was glad he and Bridget had stayed.

Lady Linton's friend, Lady Bell, was far more interested in her champagne and giggling with her friends to be taking any notice of her own score, let alone how other players were adding theirs. When she lost handsomely, she simply shrugged and ordered another drink from a footman.

Now there is a woman without money issues.

Stephen leaned across to Bridget. "I think we might be

able to forget about her wanting to take money from your mother."

They had achieved at least something this evening—one suspect could be removed. But Stephen wasn't satisfied. At this rate, it would take them days, possibly weeks to cull names from the list.

His gaze drifted from the card table to the people gathered around. For every game, there was a good number of guests just watching. Some paying particular attention to every hand.

What if our blackmailer isn't a card player? What if they are someone who likes to watch and over time figured out Lady Linton's trick?

"Can you recall what the original note said?" he asked.

"Something about seeing Mama adding up her tally wrong. Why?" replied Bridget.

He rose and offered her his hand. There was little point in them lingering at the party any longer. And they needed to talk. "I think that might be enough for this evening. Let me escort you home."

The instant their fingers touched; a thrill of need sent all thoughts of lists fleeing from Stephen's mind. A sensible man would have let go as soon as Bridget had got to her feet, but he didn't. Instead, he was rooted to the spot staring at her.

At those blue eyes in which he was certain the unmistakable glaze of lust shone.

She is as affected by my touch as I am hers. This is dangerous territory.

"If you like, we could share a glass of wine at my home. We could go over our thoughts from this evening and make further plans. I have a well-rounded Shiraz I think you might enjoy," she said.

"That would be very nice. You can even take a pencil and put a strike through Lady Bell's name," he replied.

Stephen couldn't care less about the wine or the list. He just wanted to get Bridget alone.

Chapter Thirteen

To her relief, only one footman was waiting in the foyer when Bridget and Stephen made it back to Berkeley Square. Dismissing him as quickly as possible, she led Stephen upstairs.

He was right on her heels when she stepped into the drawing room. He closed the door swiftly behind him and turned the key in the lock.

His large frame filled her entire field of vision as she turned to face him. She sensed a momentary hint of danger but quickly pushed all worries aside. For this man's touch, she would risk it all.

"Bridget."

Just hearing him speak her name in such a sultry manner had heat pooling in her loins. Her nipples pressed hard against the fabric of her chemise. And from the look on his face, it was clear that Stephen was standing right alongside her on the edge of desire. Any moment now he would take hold of her hand, and together they would leap into the abyss.

His fingertips brushed over her cheek and he smiled. "You

are blushing again. Tell me, Bridget, what is it that has your blood so heated?"

She swallowed deeply. "You. Every time you look at me, I ache for your touch."

A large hand cupped the back of her head, and he leaned in, placing a soft, barely there, kiss on her lips. Bridget shivered as a frisson of lust raced down her spine. It was still tingling in her toes when Stephen leaned in and kissed her a second time.

This kiss, while still tender, was more certain. More controlled. His lips worked slowly over hers, gentle at first, almost as if he were asking for her permission. For a man of such determined action, this was most unexpected, but also very welcome.

She was no wilting and timid virgin. In her first year or so of marriage, Bridget had experienced many long afternoons of passionate lovemaking. She knew exactly what she wanted from a man—what she craved from Stephen.

He blazed a trail of hot, delicious kisses down the side of her neck. Bridget groaned.

His hands settled on the front of her gown, lightly cupping her breasts. Her already firm nipples instantly peaked, aching for his attention. When his thumb stroked over the hardened bud, she trembled.

Thank heavens I wore my light stays.

She was still fully invested in the kiss when Stephen broke it off and took a hurried step back. "We shouldn't be doing this. It isn't right."

All of Bridget's hopes for a night of wild, passionate sex evaporated in an instant. Her lust-fired body cooled.

He doesn't want me.

Stephen slowly shook his head. "Don't get the wrong idea, Bridget. I don't mean we shouldn't ever share a bed. Lord knows you are a beautiful and tempting woman. It's just that the timing is not right. You are my client. I don't sleep with people who are paying me. I am a rake not a fancy man."

"I understand, and that makes perfect sense. I would never wish for you to feel that you were anything other than a full partner in any sexual encounter," she replied.

What a pity. I might struggle to pay for the coal, but I could easily find the money to keep you at my beck and call. My own private fancy man.

Her wicked thoughts were shameful, but Bridget didn't care. She wanted Stephen to know that she desired him. That she was prepared to bend or break as many rules as possible to get him into her bed. "So, if I was not your client, you would consider a relationship with me?"

"Yes and no. Once we get this case closed, I am open to you and me sharing your bed. But as for a relationship, that is completely out of the question. I am not seeking a long-term lover. We have one night together, and, in the morning, you shall find me gone."

Of course, he wasn't offering anything more than a discrete liaison. He was Sir Stephen Moore, master of the ballroom *and* the bedroom. While she was the *Barren Baroness*, and most men wouldn't consider her to be anything other than a short-term carnal conquest.

But isn't that what you want? No strings attached. And no one crushing your heart because you cannot give him a child. Naomi was right. You should take a chance.

She held out her hand. "I agree to those terms. When this is all over, you and I shall spend one night together. A shared passionate embrace with no boundaries, and—no breakfast."

He glanced at her outstretched fingers, and for a moment Bridget wondered if he might have changed his mind.

"Good," he said.

And then he kissed her all over again.

Chapter Fourteen

They agreed to meet again the following morning. Time was of the essence, and apart from crossing Lady Bell off the list, they hadn't actually made a great deal of progress in the past few days.

Bridget resisted the sensible notion of heading up to bed after Stephen finally left in the early hours of the morning. Her mind and heart were still in too much of a state of flux. The tall, fair-haired rogue had stirred so many things within her that she had thought long dead, that Bridget found herself unable to consider sleep.

If I am going to stay up, I may as well make use of my time.

She retrieved her mother's diary and cribbage notebook from the bookcase and settled by the fire to read. It wasn't until she had read forty pages of the diary before sleep finally caught up with her. Bridget's fitful dream featured a shop full of modistes who sewed gowns made entirely out of cribbage cards, while clusters of people gathered around to watch.

When she woke, just before the dawn, she sat upright in the chair and attempted to stretch. Her neck was a tired knot. She winced as she rolled her stiff and cranky shoulders, trying to loosen them. As she shifted, papers crinkled under her foot. She glanced down.

The diary and notebook had fallen on the floor, and she was now standing on them. Bridget bent and picked up the notebook. As she did, several pages came loose and flittered onto the carpet.

She sighed. Her mother had entrusted these private possessions to her keep, and instead of taking care of them, she had torn them apart.

"Mama will not be pleased."

Her interest stirred as she collected the pages. They were a different thickness to the rest of the notebook.

When she opened the first of them, Bridget's curiosity quickly turned to deep concern. Spread before her was a rather risqué drawing of her mother. Lady Linton had been sketched reclining fully naked on a chaise lounge.

With her heart racing, Bridget opened the other pages. They were all detailed drawings of her mother in various states of undress.

I wonder if Papa knows about these. If he doesn't, Mama and I will be having stern words. How reckless can you be?

Wasn't it bad enough that someone other than her father had been permitted to see the countess naked? The fact that she had then allowed them to draw her made it all the more scandalous. What was her mother thinking?

When she got to the last drawing, her quiet hope that she had seen the worst of her mother's secrets was quickly dashed. The picture itself was bad enough, but what had been written on the other side of the page brought Bridget to the verge of tears.

Lady Linton had kept a tally of the money she had won as a result of cheating during recent weeks. And to top it all off, she had also included the names of the people she had duped.

Her worries turned to deep concern as she took in the names. Some she knew quite well, while others were mere acquaintances. But only one was on both the list of her mother's victims and Stephen's roll of suspects.

The Duchess of Redditch. Lady Kitty Steele. Naomi's mother.

Doing her utmost to hold her rising panic at bay, Bridget quickly penned a note to Stephen.

Within half an hour, a barely awake footman was headed out the door and on his way to Gracechurch Street.

Had Lady Linton pushed her old friend one step too far and now the duchess was seeking revenge? And what of Stephen? How would he handle it if the blackmailer transpired to be someone he held in high regard?

Bridget sat head in hands at her writing desk, praying with all her might that she was wrong. If she wasn't, then two of the most well-known and respected families of the *ton* were about to become the center of the biggest scandal of the year.

And all over a stupid card game.

Chapter Fifteen

When the Vatican next called for prospective saints, Stephen was going to put Lady Alice Steele's name up for consideration. She never said no whenever he asked her to mind Toby. Overnight stays at Harry and Alice's house were so regular, that the young boy had his own dedicated room.

With Toby yet again sleeping at number 16 Grosvenor Street, Stephen was able to make his way over to Bridget's house a little after dawn. Her note had left him shaken. The naked pictures of Lady Linton were one thing, but the mere thought that Kitty Steele could possibly be the blackmailer had thrown him.

The pensive mood he was in as he stepped into Bridget's drawing room was in stark contrast to that which he had been enjoying when he left the previous evening. The memory of holding Bridget in his arms while he kissed her was now replaced by fear.

He closed the door behind him, and Bridget hurried into his embrace. They shared a brief, comforting kiss before she pulled away. The disappointment which came with the loss of her touch took him by surprise.

His fingers itched to stroke her soft hair, to brush against the warm skin of her rosy cheeks the same as they had done the previous night.

"Thank you for coming. I didn't know what to do, but I just couldn't wait until later in the morning to talk to you," she said.

"You were right to send for me. We have to move expeditiously on any clues that come our way," he replied.

She pointed toward the occasional table which sat in between the two sofas. There was a piece of paper on the top. "Look at it and tell me if I am wrong in what I am thinking."

Stephen took a seat and picked up the paper. His brows knitted as he took in the detailed sketch of Lady Linton. While it was not something he would ever have expected to see, he had to hand it to the artist—they were skilled with a pen and ink.

"Turn it over and read the back."

He did as Bridget asked, and his heart immediately sank. Lady Kitty Steele suddenly went from the bottom of the list of suspects, all the way to the top. She had plenty of motive. She had the means and, of course, knowing Lady Linton as well as she did, she had the opportunity.

He gritted his teeth, holding back a long string of expletives.

It was ironic that Kitty's son, Harry, was the member of the rogues of the road who had the most experience in handling scandals. Before his marriage to Alice, he had made a nice living out of managing other people's missteps.

What will he do if it's his mother who is involved?

"I know Lady Steele and my mother are good friends. I would hate to end their relationship over this, but the evidence against the duchess is compelling," said Bridget.

Stephen had known the Duchess of Redditch since he was a boy. She had never shown the slightest inkling of having a spiteful bone in her body. If there was anyone, he could trust to give an honest answer, it was Kitty.

Please don't let me be wrong about her. It would kill Harry.

"Bridget, please go and get your hat and cloak. I think it is time we paid a visit to Redditch House. If the duchess is the blackmailer, I would prefer that we confront her in private. If there is going to be damage, we need to do all we can to mitigate it. Can you just imagine the almighty row that will flare up if this becomes public?"

Not to mention that Harry would most certainly never forgive Stephen if he threw Kitty to the wolves.

Chapter Sixteen

The Duchess of Redditch set the sketch of Lady Linton on the table and sat back in her chair. Placing her hands together, she considered both Bridget and Stephen over steepled fingers. She didn't seem the least bit fazed in having discovered that she was on the list of possible blackmailers. "I can fully understand why you might think me the villain. But I can assure you I am not. In fact, I'm the one who referred Tristan to you, Stephen."

Bridget let out a large sigh of relief. They may not have uncovered 'N', but at least her mother's relationship with the duchess remained intact. "I am so sorry for all of this."

Kitty nodded. "So am I. Your mother has been cheating me at cribbage for years—so long that it has become somewhat of a private joke between us. She does make good on the money each Christmas. I think she sees it as her way of recalibrating the clocks on an annual basis."

"Not exactly how one should treat their closest and most trusted friends," observed Stephen.

The duchess raised an eyebrow. "Tell that to the Duke of Monsale the next time he takes a large cut out of the proceeds of one of your jobs. At least Lady Linton is honest with me about her little game."

Bridget flinched at the remark, but Stephen merely studied the cuffs of his jacket sleeves. She had heard rumors of how, since he had taken on the title, Andrew McNeal had transformed the previously near bankrupt Duchy of Monsale into one of the wealthiest in all of England. The specifics as to how he had managed this accomplishment were by all accounts a tightly held secret.

But these people appear to know. Curious.

Stephen cleared his throat. "We have taken up enough of your time, your grace. Perhaps it is best that Lady Bridget and I should leave."

The duchess snorted. "We have only just got started. I know you well enough, Stephen Moore, that I won't have been the only one on your list of suspects. Hand it over."

She clicked her fingers imperiously in his direction, and Bridget didn't know where to look. Or whether to laugh. Stephen didn't strike her as the sort of man used to taking orders from anyone, let alone a woman.

He fished in his jacket pocket and after producing the list, handed it over.

Kitty perused it for a moment, making strange faces as she read each name out aloud. "I must say I am disappointed in both the names and the paucity of the list. I hope you are not taking Bridget's money for this job because if you are, you should hand it back."

"I . . . I," stammered Stephen.

The duchess tossed the list onto a nearby table. "The women above the rank of baroness can go immediately. None of them need the blunt. The same goes for the new money ladies; they are trying to claim a spot in society, not tear it down."

Stephen picked up the note and, taking a pencil, put a line

through every single name. In one fell swoop, all the suspects were cleared. He sat back in his chair and sighed.

They had to start all over again.

Or perhaps not.

"What about the men? I've just noticed that there were only women on the list," said Bridget.

Lady Steele nodded. "Now that is possibly a more fertile piece of ground. I know of at least one gentleman who mixes in our circles and is circumspect with his spending to the point of being tightfisted. And I don't think it is by choice but rather financial circumstance."

Seated side by side on the sofa, Bridget and Stephen both leaned forward. "Who?" they asked in unison.

Kitty turned the page with the cribbage list over and pointed at the nude sketch of Lady Linton. "The man who drew this picture. Lionel Hosey. He is often at functions and parties, always lurking around the ladies and paying them sweet compliments. He tried it once with me, but I gave him short shrift. I understand his formal employment is with M. Jones, the former editor of *The Scourge* over in Bond Street. These private portraits are extra income for him, but his main job is to create illustrations for the public to buy."

Lionel Hosey had a particular reputation among the women of the *ton* for not only being well-endowed but knowing exactly what do to with his gift. There were whispers of him possessing special talents. He had at one time been on Bridget's private list of potential lovers.

Not that I am going to tell either of these people.

She hadn't been aware that Mister Hosey was the gentleman artist behind *those* pictures. Now that Bridget knew he had seen her mother naked, he most certainly wouldn't be getting anywhere near her.

After picking up the notebook, Bridget retrieved the remaining pieces of folded paper which had been stuffed into the back and laid them out on the table. Stephen had to know the full story of her mother's connection to the illustrator.

"Mister Hosey also did these for Mama," she said.

Lady Linton had always had a soft spot for struggling artists. She claimed that paying them to create pieces for her was a form of artistic charity. Little wonder Lionel Hosey had found his way to convince her to pose for him.

"He certainly presents an interesting view of the world," said Stephen.

An embarrassed Bridget went to pick up the drawings. She hated herself for having shown them to him, worried that he would judge her mother as being a foolish and unscrupulous woman.

Stephen placed his hand on hers. "Wait. We haven't discounted Lionel Hosey as a potential suspect. In fact, I think he should go to the top of the list."

The duchess nodded. "Poor struggling artist, watching rich women from the sidelines as they gamble money he will never have. I would suggest he is a prime candidate for a spot of blackmail."

Stephen clasped his hands together. "This is really useful information. While Bridget and I were sitting observing some card games at a party last night, I started thinking about who else could go on our list. It is clear we need to look beyond just those seated at the cribbage table."

"Come to think of it, I can imagine it wouldn't take much for someone who was paying close attention to be able to spot when someone wasn't counting properly. I wondered why you had turned to watching the watchers before we left," said Bridget.

"I meant to raise that with you last night, but we got distracted," he replied.

Lady Steele gave a not-so-subtle cough before reaching for her cup of tea.

Stephen got to his feet. "Thank you for your time this

morning, your grace. It has, as always, been illuminating." He turned to Bridget. "I shall go and say a quick hello to his grace before we leave. I won't be a moment."

As soon as he was gone, Lady Steele fixed Bridget with a sly smile. "I am not going to ask what possibly could have got the two of you distracted last night, though I can just imagine it was more than cards. I couldn't help but notice Stephen giving you the occasional small glance, my dear. And I must say, you make quite a sweet pair. Shall I start looking for a new hat to wear at a future wedding?"

Bridget shook her head. "I think you know as well as I do, your grace, that Sir Stephen Moore considers himself not to be the marrying kind."

The duchess softly chuckled. "So do all men before they succumb to cupid's arrows. Trust me, even rogues like Stephen eventually fall."

Chapter Seventeen

After leaving Redditch House, Bridget and Stephen walked the short distance from Grosvenor Street to Bond Street arm in arm. It was a warm day; the sun was shining. With Stephen beside her, Bridget found herself indulging in a private fantasy that they were husband and wife out for their regular morning stroll.

When he leaned in and smiled at her, Bridget's heart skipped a beat. The Duchess of Redditch's comment about Stephen eventually succumbing to marriage kept rolling around in her head.

Why couldn't I have married a man like you? You would have made a far better husband than Rupert.

If it were not for the heavily pregnant woman and small boy who suddenly appeared in front of them from out of a bookshop, she would have happily continued with her musings of a life that could never be.

"Sir Stephen," the boy hailed him.

Stephen turned to Bridget. "Toby and Lady Alice Steele."

Bridget caught the look of joy on the young lad's face. He was clearly not intimated by the size difference between him and Stephen.

Small children like you.

Despite his attempts to pretend he didn't care, the grin on Stephen's lips gave him away. The boy was important to him.

"Lady Alice Steele, may I present Lady Bridget Dyson," said Stephen.

Alice narrowed her eyes at him. "Isn't that supposed to be the other way around? Bridget was born a lady, whereas I only have my title due to marriage."

Bridget chortled. Someone had been studying their social etiquette guide. She held out a hand to Alice. "I think you might be the more senior on account of being married to the son of a duke, whereas . . . oh, never mind. It is a pleasure to meet you. Lady Naomi has told me so much about the lovely girl her brother had the good fortune to wed."

"And good sense," replied Alice.

Toby let go of Alice's hand and rushed over to Stephen. He held out a brown paper parcel tied up with string. He buzzed with excitement. "Lady Alice bought me books with pictures in them. Will you read them to me tonight? Please?"

Stephen nodded. "As long as you have practiced your letters, we can read the book."

Alice slipped a second parcel out from under her arm and handed it to Stephen.

"We also got Toby some more clothes. His new boots are on order for the end of the week. I shall let you and Harry settle up the matter of the accounts."

A rosy patch appeared on Stephen's cheeks. "What would I do without you Alice?"

"I would walk about town naked and barefoot," replied the boy.

Bridget stared at her boots, doing her best not to laugh. Clearly Toby had heard that remark from someone, and it wouldn't take much to guess who.

Stephen muttered something under his breath. Alice stepped forward and put a hand on his arm. "Sorry, I didn't realize he had picked up on that. I will watch my tongue around him in the future."

"You are right. I could not even begin to consider myself a passable guardian. I promise, here in front of an independent witness, that I shall make an extra effort to be more observant of Toby's needs," he replied.

"Noted," said Bridget.

The young boy clearly thought the world of Stephen. And as far as Bridget was concerned, any encouragement that she could offer to make sure that the affection was reciprocated would be well worth her time.

He is not as bad as he thinks. If he was, Toby wouldn't be so keen to have his approval.

"Are you headed home?" asked Alice.

Stephen glanced over at Bridget. "No, we have an appointment to attend. Lady Bridget and I are on company business."

Alice nodded, but said nothing. From the look which passed between her and Stephen, Bridget concluded that Harry's wife knew not to press for further information. "We shalt hold you up any longer. Will Toby be staying with Harry and I again this evening?"

Stephen screwed up his face. "I can come and collect him, but it will be late if I do. How about I come to your house for breakfast in the morning and then take him home?"

Alice met Bridget's gaze, but her words were directed at the large man standing in their midst. "I have bought Toby clothes and books, but only you can give him what he really needs."

After Alice and Toby had continued on their way, Stephen remained, slowly shaking his head. "I am still not certain that bringing him to London was the best thing I could have done."

"Does Toby know who you are? I mean, the true nature of your relationship?" she asked.

"No. I am just a stranger who suddenly appeared in his life and took him away from the only home he has ever known. I don't know when or how I am going to explain to him that he is actually my brother."

At least that went some of the way to explaining Stephen's reluctance to connect with Toby. For a large, strong male, he seemed almost timid around the boy—unsure of how he should respond to the open warmth of a child.

Is that because you have never had a loving relationship with anyone in your life?

"What did Alice mean by only you could give Toby what he really needs?" she asked, genuinely intrigued.

He sighed. "She means the boy needs a mother, and the only way he is going to get anything remotely resembling one is if I marry. And therein lies the problem."

Because you have sworn to never take on a wife.

"You made a vow not to marry and have a family. Can I tell you something, Stephen? Vows are funny things. Sometimes we don't realize how high the cost is of trying to hold true to them, until we have to pay."

Chapter Eighteen

The print seller and publisher, M. Jones's office and shopfront were located at 146 Bond Street. The front window was full of caricatures and rather scandalous drawings, which of course meant it drew quite the crowd. People were gathered tightly together whispering, pointing, and sniggering at the pictures.

A steady stream of customers filed in and out the front door of the shop. While the periodical *The Scourge* had recently closed, Mister Jones was obviously still running a lucrative business catering to the whims and amusement of the people of London.

Bridget and Stephen finally managed to fight their way through the throng to take up a spot at the window. The first thing that struck Bridget was the depth of detail in the drawings. Lionel Hosey might well be their primary suspect for blackmailer, but there was no doubting his talent.

Beside her, Stephen snorted a laugh. He pointed to a drawing over toward the left-hand side of the window. Bridget nodded. It was a caricature of a well-known lord pinching the oversized ass of a woman, while a second man stood close by and protested. She immediately recognized all three of the people in the sketch as well as the infamous scandal which their ménage à trois had caused in high society.

Thank god they didn't draw me. I would have been crushed to know that people came and made fun of my failure.

She leaned in closer, reading the speech bubble which had been drawn coming out of the lord's mouth. He was protesting his innocence of any misdeeds, while at the same time complaining that the bed the three of them had slept in was too small. It was all too ridiculous.

Bridget's gaze took in the rest of the drawing, and she was about to turn away when she caught sight of something which sent her heart straight to her mouth. She clutched at Stephen's coat sleeve. He leaned in, and she whispered in his ear, "Look—at the bottom of the picture. Can you see the figure of the archbishop and what he is saying to them? You know what that means, don't you?"

He pressed his face against the glass. "Yes. I see it. And it means that someone was careless when he wrote the letter to your mother."

When Stephen drew back, Bridget looked at the picture once more. There was no mistaking the familiar words and signature.

It is time to pay for your sins.
N.

They had discovered the blackmailer.

Chapter Nineteen

Despite Bridget's vehement protests, declaring that she wished to go immediately inside the shop and confront the owner about his employee, they left Bond Street soon after. She even offered to march upstairs and drag Lionel Hosey out from his lodgings, into the street, and give him a sound public flogging.

Stephen, of course, wasn't having any of it.

A showdown was the last thing he wanted. The resultant scandal would not only stand to ruin Bridget, but it would jeopardize his future business dealings. His whole livelihood depended on him being able to handle his client's problems with discretion.

It took quite an effort for him to haul her away from the print shop. "Let us discuss this in private. I suggest we go to your house," he said.

As they headed up the street, she fumed at him. "I can't believe you made me leave. How much more evidence do you need?"

He stopped suddenly and rounded on her. This was his case, and he was going to take charge. He angrily wagged a finger in Bridget's face. "You will hold your tongue. I am not going to go stomping around accusing a man of blackmail until I am certain he is the perpetrator. I don't have the time nor money to be fighting a legal suit brought against me for slander. You are paying me to handle this matter—let me do my job."

Bridget huffed. "I've a good mind to terminate our contract here and now. What are you going to do about him? And don't you dare tell me I must stay silent. This scoundrel has threatened my family."

He held his breath and counted to five. "Can we please go to your house and talk about this where the rest of London cannot overhear? I am not trying to undermine you, Bridget. In fact, at this very moment it is *you* who is putting this whole operation in jeopardy."

To his bone-deep relief, his words seem to finally hit home. Stephen followed a seething Bridget all the way back to Berkley Square and in the front door of her house.

She was angry, blisteringly so. And for some unknown reason—it turned him on. As he followed Bridget up the stairs to her drawing room, Stephen was forced to stuff his hands into his coat pockets. His fingers were itching to grab a hold of her delightfully rounded ass and pull her hard against him.

And if she slapped him, that would be even better.

The moment the door was closed behind them, and they were in private, his lust-filled thoughts of what he wanted to do to Bridget quickly fled.

"Do you have any idea?" she cried, then promptly burst into tears.

She attempted to bat his hand away as he drew close, but Stephen was a big man, and her efforts did little. As his strong arms wrapped around her, Bridget's head fell forward, and she buried her face in the front of Stephen's coat.

Women crying all over him was an occupational hazard. He had dealt with this situation many times before. But the emotions which she stirred within him were not the usual ones. His well-practiced efforts at kind indifference failed.

Why does she get to me this way? I have always been impervious to the emotions of feeble females. But I've absolutely no defense against this. I am the one left struggling.

He rested his head on top of hers. Bridget was far from weak. Her brother would not have chosen her for the task if she had not been up to saving their family.

So, this is what family loyalty is truly about—putting everyone ahead of yourself, sacrificing all for the greater good. I don't understand why you would do it.

Bridget eventually fell silent, her breathing returning to a steady, even rhythm. When she drew back, Stephen reluctantly loosened his hold. "I don't have personal experience of what it feels like to know that someone is trying to do harm to those whom you love. I have little to no understanding of what a family is, but what I do have is years of dealing with these sorts of situations. Of solving my client's problems without them getting hurt. I don't want you hurt, Bridget. It would kill me."

She met his gaze and slowly nodded. *Good.*

"I'm sorry I reacted the way I did. I just want this over with," she replied.

He held out his hand, and after a moment's hesitation she took it. Stephen raised her fingers to his lips and placed a soft kiss on them. "This is what we are going to do. Tonight, you and I will be attending one of the regular parties where cribbage games are played. From what we now know of Lionel Hosey, there is every chance he will also be a guest."

"And then what?" she replied.

"Bridget, do you trust me?" he asked.

She sighed. "Yes, of course."

"Good. You and I are going to sit and watch this evening. If Hosey is indeed the blackmailer, which, I think, is quite likely, then observing will give us enough evidence to move against him."

Bridget frowned. It was obvious that in her court of opinion, Lionel Hosey had already been tried, convicted, and the hangman was just waiting to place the noose around his neck. But Stephen was slower when it came to passing final judgement. A mistake made at the eleventh hour could well be costly.

"I am going to tell you something that happened to Harry a little while ago. Before he married Alice, he used to be in the business of managing scandals. It was quite a lucrative career. But one day he was too rash when it came to closing out a contract, and he made a grave error. It cost an innocent man his life."

The tragic event had haunted all the rogues of the road ever since. No one wished to see such a terrible thing ever repeated.

If things went according to plan, they would know the truth about Lionel Hosey within a matter of hours. The price of success was to be patient and sure.

She managed a wan smile. "When I first saw your business card, I was perplexed. Now that I know you and how you deal with clients, I understand about the words you have printed on it. Discretion and results. It is all someone like me should ask of you, and it is precisely what you promise to deliver."

"Bridget, I have always been honest with you. I won't ever try to offer more than what I am prepared to give. That goes for both our business arrangement and anything which comes after."

"I know."

Her words said one thing, but from the way she looked at him, Stephen sensed Bridget would beg him to tell her all the pretty lies her heart wanted to hear.

He could never do that to her. His truth might be painful, but at least it was honest.

Chapter Twenty

He must be a magnificent lover. There can be no other reason why all these women are staring at him.

The lust-filled glances that were shot at Stephen from every direction as they arrived at the party later that night had Bridget gritting her teeth. She could have sworn she heard the flutter of eyelashes being batted. And if come-hither looks had a voice, it would be a dull roar.

Her faint hopes that the experience of the first time she had appeared with Stephen in public might have been an anomaly were quickly dashed. Women hungered for him.

They are not even attempting to be subtle.

He leaned in and whispered in her ear, "Ignore them. We have more important things to consider. Besides, you are with me, which means to all intents and purposes we are together."

Stephen placed his hand in the small of Bridget's back, and it was all she could not to grin. He was hers for the evening, and the other women were just going to have to keep their distance. And while it was good to have a man beside her, she resisted the temptation to once more indulge in a private fantasy of them being a real couple.

This is just for show.

Their progress into the ballroom came to a sudden halt when an elegant raven-haired matron stepped in front of Stephen. She placed a hand on his chest and dramatically sighed. "My dearest Stephen, when I heard of your recent loss, I was devastated. You poor man."

Bridget held her nerve, doing everything not to show the slightest hint of jealousy over the woman's behavior. Stephen Moore was an imposing, handsome specimen of the male species. It was natural that he attracted attention. She just wished it didn't bother her as much as it did.

"Thank you for your kind words. Would you please excuse us?" he replied.

He grabbed a hold of Bridget's hand and dragged her toward the nearest exit leading out into the garden. Once outside, he kept walking. They were well away from the rest of the gathering when Stephen finally stopped. "That woman . . ." he began.

"Is none of my business. I understand how this works. You don't need to explain yourself to me," she replied.

Their gazes met, but instead of the usual calm look on his face, he appeared flustered. Dare she think embarrassed?

"I had a brief liaison with her some time ago. I made my position clear both before and after, but unfortunately some ladies find it difficult to take 'no' for an answer."

"Of course." Bridget hated the edge of disappointment in her voice. She might not appreciate the woman throwing herself in front of Stephen in such a public way, but she could understand it. What she couldn't fully accept was why he was so determined to keep a real relationship at bay.

"Affairs create expectations, and I cannot fulfil any of them," he replied.

"So, you just sample the delights of female company but never stay for the main course?"

Stephen's brows furrowed.

I have offended him.

Bridget drew back. "I'm sorry. That was unkind. I have no right to judge you on your life choices. We barely know one another."

The furrow deepened. He wasn't taking this at all well.

She turned, intending to head inside, but Stephen took a hold of her arm, pulling her back to him. "No, we don't know one another well. And I think it is something we should remedy."

He lowered his head so that their faces were a hair's breadth from touching.

"I am not boasting when I say that there are a hundred other women in that ballroom who, if given half a chance, would take your place right now. But I don't want any of them. Only you, Bridget."

If she was the only woman he desired, he should prove it.

"Kiss me," she whispered.

He slipped an arm around her waist, drawing her to him. "Your wish is my command."

Chapter Twenty-One

With the taste of her kiss still on his lips, Stephen accompanied Bridget back inside the party. The perils of mixing business with pleasure threatened to addle his mind. It was impossible to think about the job at hand when his lust-starved body was gently thrumming with need. Need for Bridget.

"I suggest we split up and observe the goings-on this evening from different vantage points. As a couple, I think we create too much interest," he said.

A beautiful widow and one of the *ton's* avowed bachelors being seen together was always going to raise an eyebrow or two. Under other circumstances Stephen might not have minded, but tonight he wanted to be the one doing the watching.

"I don't want Lionel Hosey seeing us and beginning to wonder about our connection. We arrived together, but we should spend as much time as we can apart."

Bridget nodded her agreement. "Yes, we must avoid giving him any cause for concern. I shall take a seat over in the far corner. As I am just reentering society, people will expect me to be circumspect and not dance."

A flash of anger hit him.

What right does society have in making a woman submit to such a long period of mourning, especially over a man who made a point of humiliating her in public.

The idea of Bridget sitting neglected and alone was wrong. She was the sort of woman who should be center stage and shining. If she was his, he would never allow her to hide her light.

If she was mine?

His gaze remained fixed on Bridget as she walked away. They had kissed twice now. He yearned to set his lips all over her naked body. Desire for her simmered beneath his skin. Stephen took a long, slow breath in, doing his best to calm his burning primal urges.

When his gaze fell on Lionel Hosey, he almost sighed with relief. Dealing with the blackmailer was a welcome distraction from his growing obsession with Bridget.

Time to go to work.

With a glass of brandy in hand, Stephen slowly made his way around the room. When he passed the spot where Bridget was seated, he gave the barest of nods in her direction. Anyone who happened to see them would think nothing of it.

Finally, he settled in the spot he had chosen the moment he and Bridget had arrived. A comfortable sofa against the wall, partly occupied by a snoozing, aged dowager. It was the perfect place to not only watch the card games and their players, but also those guests who were merely spectators.

To his left was a cluster of chairs. Seated on the one closest to him was his prey. Lionel Hosey.

It didn't take long for Stephen's interest in the gentleman to reach fever pitch. While the other guests drank and happily chatted while watching the game, Lionel's focus was firmly on the cards and the players.

When Lionel slipped a notebook out of his jacket pocket,

Stephen sat forward. The sketch artist jotted down a few words before putting the book away.

Sly dog. I wonder what you are writing in your little book.

This ritual continued for some time. While Lionel watched the players, and occasionally took notes, Stephen kept a weathered eye on him.

I bet you are looking for your next victim. Someone else who you can blackmail.

He doubted that Lady Linton was the only target of Lionel Hosey's moneymaking scheme. Gambling was rife within the *ton*, with fortunes regularly won and lost. Bridget's mother would most certainly not be alone in her miscounting of the cards. The field was wide open for anyone who had in mind to seek payment for their silence.

The old lady next to Stephen on the sofa stirred from her sleep. She stared at him. "Good evening," he said.

"If I had known that falling asleep was all it took to get a giant, handsome specimen such as yourself to keep my company, I would have started snoozing at parties long ago," she said.

Stephen got to his feet. He bowed to the dowager. "Someone has to look after Sleeping Beauty, but I am afraid I am not the prince whose kiss you seek. I am still a frog bound by enchantment."

She wagged a finger in his direction. "Ah, so it is you who needs the kiss of a fair lady to save him."

He chuckled softly.

It would take more than a simple kiss to break the curse.

Across the room, he caught Bridget's eye and pointed in the direction of the garden. She followed him outside.

Away from the other guests, they huddled in close.

"I've been observing Lionel Hosey for an hour, and he is definitely watching the players rather than the games. He has been taking notes all evening too. I think it is time to make a move against him," said Stephen.

Bridget nodded. "Yes, from where I was seated, I could see that he made no effort to engage in conversation with anyone. He also appeared to be taking great interest in one lady who has been consistently winning all night. I wonder if he has decided she is also cheating and might be worthy of extortion."

"Who is to say that your mother is his only victim."

"So, what now?"

This was the part of the contract where Stephen would strike out on his own, his client taking a step back, well out of harm's way. "I think it is time you went home. I shall wait until our friend leaves the party and then go have a word with him."

"Can't I come with you? I would like very much to confront this blackguard," replied Bridget.

Stephen shook his head. "When I said I was going to have a word with Mister Hosey, I meant a firm word. Sometimes that message has to be delivered in a way that is not suitable for others to observe, if you get my meaning."

This was dangerous work, and while he would love to be able to indulge Bridget's desire to come face to face with the man who threatened her family, Stephen was not going to ever put her safety in question. She would have to settle, as his many other clients had done, with his reassurances that the matter had been dealt with and was now over.

"Alright, but could you please send word as soon as you can? I won't sleep a wink until I know this nightmare is at an end," replied Bridget.

Another party guest passed close by, and Stephen waited until they were out of earshot. He leaned in. "I can go one better. If things are resolved tonight, I shall call upon you in the morning."

"No. Tonight. I will wait up for you."

He hesitated for a moment, unsure of how to respond. Her words could be construed in several ways. Was she just going to remain awake to hear his news or was there something else? An offer, perhaps. If he closed the case tonight, Bridget wouldn't be his client any longer.

And you wouldn't be mixing business with pleasure.

"Let's leave now. The sooner I have dealt with Lionel Hosey, the quicker I can be at your place. After that, we can talk," he said.

She placed a hand on his chest, and her piercing blue eyes met his. "Stay safe and come back to me. I need you."

As Bridget walked away, Stephen pondered her last words. He couldn't ever remember a time when a woman had needed him.

Want, yes. Need, never.

Chapter Twenty-Two

When Lionel Hosey finally left the party, Stephen followed him all the way back to Bond Street. He stopped a few yards away as Lionel passed through the entrance which led up to the apartment above the printer's shop.

He had just taken a step forward, checking the street, when a figure in a hooded black cloak appeared from out of the shadows.

"I changed my mind."

Bridget?

"What are you doing? I thought we agreed you would go home, and we would talk later," he said.

"We did, but I decided that I am sick of being made to sit on the edge of my life without having a say in its future. I am coming with you," she replied.

Taking her firmly by the arm, he hauled her farther up the street and into the doorway of a nearby shop. "No. I am not having you put in danger."

She shook herself free of his hold. "You said yourself that Lionel Hosey was an amateur. I doubt very much that a man who wields a sketchbook and ink for a living is going to pose any real risk."

"I don't care what you think, my answer is no."

"So be it. I am formally ending our contract. Thank you for your time, Sir Stephen. I shall take things from here."

She was serious, he was gob smacked.

"And just how do you propose to get him to confess that he is the blackmailer?" There clearly couldn't be any substance to her bravado. He just had to hold firm and make Bridget see sense.

She slipped a hand into the folds of her cloak and produced a pistol.

His reflexes kicked in, and Stephen quickly seized her by the wrist, snatching the weapon from her fingers. "Where the devil did you get a double-barrelled flintlock from?"

"Rupert had quite a collection of guns. He was always out hunting. My job was to patch him and his friends up when they accidentally shot one another. And while I didn't get to shoot all that often, I can still fire a pistol and hit the mark."

There was clearly no dissuading Bridget from her goal. A difficult choice now lay before him. He either let her go and cause whatever havoc she intended, or he took her along with him. A reluctant Stephen handed the pistol back to Bridget.

"You can come with me but keep that damn thing out of sight. Firing off a weapon should be the last thing you do. Is that clear?"

"Crystal," she replied.

His height and bulk were Stephen's usual tools for instilling fear in his prey. Only hardened criminals required the added threat of being shot to make them obey his command.

"I cannot believe you are doing this," he grumbled.

Somewhere along the way he had seriously misjudged Bridget.

So much for the wallflower widow.

"Stop complaining. You will still get paid. Now let's go and finally put an end to this farce."

Stephen was relieved when Bridget let him take the lead, and they headed back to the doorway and up the stairs to Lionel Hosey's apartment. He rapped sharply on the door.

Hosey had just opened it when Stephen put a hand in the middle of his chest and pushed him firmly back, following him into the room. Bridget remained out of sight in the hallway.

"What the devil?" cried Hosey. As he staggered back, he reached into his jacket pocket, producing a knife.

Bloody hell, why is everyone armed to the teeth this evening?

"If you think to rob me, you have the wrong person. I can and will defend myself," he said.

Stephen was a man usually able to keep his temper well under control, but after having observed Lionel Hosey's sly behavior this evening, his fists were eager to do the man great harm. The threat of a knife held little fear for him. "You are able to protect yourself. Unlike those whom you seek to blackmail and ruin," said Stephen.

Hosey's eyes narrowed. "I saw you arrive at the party this evening with Lady Bridget Dyson. Who the hell are you?"

Stephen placed his left hand over his right and cracked the knuckles. It echoed loudly in the small of the room, and he smiled. "You didn't really think Lady Linton was just going to quietly pay up, did you? She may be a naughty girl, but she isn't stupid."

Bridget stepped across the threshold and closed the door behind her. "This gentleman is the man whom I hired to deal with the problem of a dirty, disgusting blackmailer," she said.

A look crossed Hosey's face, and for a minute, it appeared as if he was going to try to deny everything. Then his shoulders slumped. "I didn't mean to hurt anyone. I just needed money. It was foolish of me to send that note, and I regret it."

Stephen clapped his hands together loudly, and Hosey jumped.

"Ah! That's more like it. You are not a well-built chap, and to be honest, the thought of pummeling you with my fists really didn't appeal. I'm not one for mismatched bouts. Especially not in front of a lady." He held out his hand, and Hosey placed the knife in Stephen's palm. The weapon instantly disappeared into the folds of Stephen's great coat.

"And the notebook," said Bridget.

With a resigned sigh, Lionel reached into his pocket and withdrew the book Stephen had observed him making notes in.

"Is that all the wicked scribblings you have?" asked Stephen.

He raised an eyebrow when Hosey frowned. The cheeky beggar had the gall to look affronted. He wasn't the least surprised. In his experience, cheats and liars didn't like their honesty being questioned.

"Yes, that is the only book. You can see that it covers quite a few weeks of the social season," Hosey replied.

"Good. You should be pleased that you are dealing with someone like me. Another gentleman would likely have summoned the authorities and had you placed in irons."

"I have given you my notes. What else can I do to make you leave?"

Stephen cleared his throat. He liked to take a moment to compose himself whenever he was about to deliver an ultimatum. It added a certain gravitas to the occasion.

"The usual. You promise to stay away from high society and, of course, Lady Linton. You make good on that promise, and we don't have any problems. If, however, you decide to try to outwit me, not only will you be ruined, but I will come for you."

He took a step forward and towered over Lionel Hosey. "I

normally add a dark threat in here about your body never being found, but I think that between the two of us, we can take that as implied. What else was there? Oh, yes. If I see you within ten feet of a cribbage table ever again, you won't have any fingers left to draw pretty pictures of naked ladies. Am I clear?"

"Yes."

"Good. Because I would hate to have to pay a visit to your employer or the authorities. You made several amateur mistakes with the blackmail note. I have more than enough evidence to see you hang."

The fear which shone in Lionel Hosey's eyes was real. The message had been well and truly received.

Stephen, however, was not yet done. "Lady Dyson, could you please give Mister Hosey and I a brief moment alone?"

Bridget glared at him but headed for the door. "I shall wait outside," she said.

Once Bridget was out of sight, Stephen stretched out his arm. Placing one of his large hands around Hosey's throat, he lifted him so that his toes were barely touching the floor. At the same time, firm pressure was applied. A minute or so later, the man's face had turned an unpleasant shade of purple.

"I hope for your sake you take heed of my words because if I ever have to come here again, I won't be so magnanimous. And I won't ask Lady Dyson to keep her pistol in its holster."

He set the blackmailer back on his feet and headed for the door. Lionel Hosey's pitiful, hacking cough followed Stephen and Bridget down the stairs.

※

Out in Bond Street once more, Stephen stopped under a streetlamp and checked his pocket watch. It was late—too late to go knocking on Harry and Alice's door to collect Toby. He made a mental note to do something nice for Alice in recognition of all her support. With a baby coming soon, he doubted he would be able to keep abusing her good nature forever.

I need to find a nanny. And a house. I can't raise him at the coaching offices.

Not only were the accommodations at Gracechurch Street rudimentary, but it also left Toby exposed to the illicit world of the rogues of the road. He was not going to raise his younger brother to be a career criminal. Toby would be educated to become a gentleman and, in time, take his place in London society.

There is enough money in the Moore family estate to provide for him.

Thoughts of his responsibilities as a guardian would have to wait until morning. It was nearing one o'clock in the morning, and Stephen wanted a drink and for him and Bridget to talk.

"Had you planned some more of this evening or was waving a pistol about in Mister Hosey's face the extent of it?" He was still angry with Bridget over her reckless behavior. Stephen wanted nothing more than to shake some sense into her. But when he caught a glimpse of her face in the pale light, he changed his mind.

Her expression spoke of a different need—of finally sating the hunger which burned between them.

"I had hoped that you might want to share this evening's victory with me. To celebrate. I am no longer your client, so our other agreement could be . . ."

For the first time in a little while, Bridget seemed unsure of herself. Almost shy. The gun-wielding matron was now replaced by a young woman wishing to be reassured that he still wanted to share her bed.

"Let us get a hack and head to Berkley Square," he said.

Reaching her home, Bridget slipped a key in the front door. There were no servants to be seen about the foyer. The message was clear—she had made certain that they were not going to be disturbed.

She held out her hand. "Come upstairs."

When they got to the top of the first landing, instead of going the usual left, Bridget turned right.

Hopefully, her bedroom is this way.

Stephen's cock gave a twitch. It was anticipating a spot of action—something it hadn't seen in a long while.

Down, boy. Wooing first.

With the coaching business, numerous trips with Gus to France, and having to deal with his father's legacy, Stephen simply had not had the time to go chasing the wicked women of the *ton*. Tonight, hopefully, his dry spell was about to come to an end.

Bridget stopped at an open doorway and ushered him in. To his disappointment, the room on the other side was not a bedroom.

Blast. I thought we were going to indulge. Perhaps I misread the signals.

His gaze settled on a long, deep-blue velvet chaise lounge and hope flared once more. Then he caught sight of the mahogany-colored leather sofa, and he was suddenly torn. Both would serve well for seduction.

So many choices. Where is a man to begin?

If things went well, then perhaps he may not have to decide between them. Bridget and he had the rest of the night ahead of them.

"Would you like a drink? I mean, we should celebrate," she said.

He nodded. "Yes, we should. Mister Hosey got the message, and so I don't think he will be troubling anyone else in society with his foolish attempts at blackmail."

Stephen pulled the knife out of his coat pocket and dropped it on a nearby table.

"A souvenir of your night of danger. But may I suggest you keep it in your stocking drawer?"

She picked the knife up and grinned at him. "I will keep it alongside the pistol."

He shook his head. "I had a horrid feeling you might say that."

After unfastening the ties of her cloak, she slipped it off her shoulders and draped it over a chair. The gentleman's holster and pistol came next.

Bridget crossed to the sideboard and soon returned to Stephen's side bearing two glasses of wine. "Here's to the successful completion of your contract, Sir Stephen," she said, handing him a drink.

As Bridget sipped her wine, Stephen's gaze remained fixed on her mouth. When she moved the glass away, her lips were moist. She licked them, and his manhood stood to attention.

He reached out and wrapping his fingers around the stem of Bridget's glass, took it from her grasp. She let him. Their drinks were set on a table next to the sofa. His gaze lingered on the mahogany leather, and he slowly blinked.

I can just imagine you naked and spread open before me on it.

Bridget moved toward him, her fingers toying with the openings of her gown.

Stephen slipped a hand about her waist and pulled her roughly to him. His cock, hard and demanding, pressed against her stomach. His blood pumped through his body at a furious rate.

I want her.

Lust and his long-neglected sexual appetite kicked into a full gallop. Bridget was his for the taking, and he was never one to disappoint a lady.

"How about we save the wine until later? If I am reading

the look on your face correctly, I don't think either of us is in the mood to sit and chat over a drink. I would much rather my lips be used to bring you pleasure. And when I say pleasure, I mean the most magnificent you have ever had."

"Stephen," she whispered.

He claimed her mouth with his.

Chapter Twenty-Three

The touch of a strong male who wanted her had Bridget sighing into Stephen's embrace. Just the chance to be held in a man's arms and be given sexual release was far more than she had known for the past four years.

I need you. I want you. And I want you to need me.

He had said he only ever spent one night with a woman, but Bridget didn't care. She would take whatever he offered. And in return, he could have her all.

Stephen was a master at kissing. He turned the simple act of two pairs of lips touching one another into something that only the poets could describe in a sonnet.

When he gently, teasingly, bit her bottom lip, Bridget almost swooned. She clung to the front of his jacket. It was all she could do to stop from falling to her knees.

He pulled back from the kiss and breathlessly whispered, "We need to slow this down. Let me take control. I have a feeling that if I give you the reins, there is every chance that this horse will bolt."

He was right. She didn't want to hold back. She wanted everything and now.

Whatever you ask, I am yours.

"What would you like me to do?" she asked.

His long, lingering gaze had her mind going to the most wicked of places. Of the things she hoped they would experience together.

"Are you comfortable with us being in this room or did you wish to retire to the bedroom?" he asked.

"I chose this room for a reason." She pointed toward the chaise lounge. "I have been imagining you and me on that for the better part of a week. If I am only going to get one night with you, Stephen, I want to experience more than just the usual."

She nodded at the leather sofa. "Or if your tastes run to something different, we could always use that. Perhaps even both."

A grinning Stephen tugged on the laces of her gown. "Come with me."

He led her over to the chaise lounge where he plonked himself in the middle of it, then arranged Bridget so that she was standing before him. A flush of heat coursed through her as his gaze ran up and down her body.

If this is the effect, he has on me while I am fully clothed, I might spontaneously combust the instant he sees me naked.

"I was going to command you to slowly strip for me, but something tells me neither of us has that amount of patience." He took hold of the sides of her skirts and lifting them, bared her lower torso and legs to his sight. "Even better than I had imagined, and believe me, I have been doing a lot of imagining."

This was utterly scandalous behavior. And she was loving it.

Stephen pushed himself off the chaise lounge and knelt on the floor. His face was level with her sex. "Just a taste before we rid you of these confounded garments," he whispered.

With her skirts bunched in his hands, he leaned forward and placed a kiss on the outer folds of Bridget's labia. She shivered with the thrill; with the anticipation of what was to come next.

"Oh," she murmured as his tongue swept from the bottom of her sex to the tip of her sensitive bud. She lay a trembling hand on his shoulder, taking a firmer hold when he delved into her heated core.

Stephen, licked, sucked, and stroked her with his tongue. Pleasure she had forgotten even existed tore through her core. She stuffed a hand into her mouth to stop from crying out.

One long lick followed by him sucking on her nib sent Bridget close to the edge. Then Stephen drew back. "Can't have you coming too soon. That would not do."

He got to his feet, wiping his face with a handkerchief he produced from his jacket pocket. Half mute with lust, Bridget simply stared at him.

"Clothes. Off. Now," he commanded.

Bridget stirred from her haze, fumbling with the openings of her gown. No sooner had she got them undone, then it was lifted over her head and tossed onto the floor. She blinked twice, unable to fathom how his coat, jacket, shirt, and trousers had all managed to magically disappear in the time it had taken her to loosen her bodice.

Stephen slowly shook his head and tutted. "You are wearing stays. They are the bane of every man's existence. Now where is a knife when you need one?"

She held up a finger. "Just a minute."

With no care for her state of semi-undress, Bridget scuttled across the floor before returning quickly with the knife Stephen had confiscated from Lionel Hosey. She held it out to him.

"It seems apt to use this to unwrap your victory prize," she said.

He flicked the switchblade open and grinned at her. "Last chance to save the undergarment."

"I am sure I can make an appointment for some new ones."

The sharp edge of the blade cut through the ties like they were butter. Stephen closed up the knife and placed it on the nearby side table. Bridget held her breath as he took hold of both sides of her stays and wrenched them apart. The poor chemise underneath never stood a chance. He tore it in two.

Cool, air kissed her nipples, and they instantly peaked.

Touch me.

"You are the most beautiful woman I have ever seen," he murmured, the thick emotion in his voice overcoming her worry that this was something he said to every woman he bedded. Stephen made her feel special. Made her want to believe that there had never been and never would be another woman for him.

Tonight, that was all that mattered.

He picked her up, and she wrapped her legs around him. Bridget clung to Stephen. When they reached the chaise lounge, he sat once more. His hard cock pressed against the opening of her sex as slowly, gently he lowered her onto him.

"Ride me," he said.

With her hands placed on either side of his shoulders, Bridget rose up and then sunk down once more. By the third time she had done this, Stephen was seated fully within her.

Her eyelids drifted closed. This was beyond anything she had ever known before. Bridget rested her forehead against his. "Just give me a moment. You are not a small man."

A rumble of laughter came from deep within his chest. "I should have mentioned that you might have difficulty walking in the morning."

His fingers traced lightly over her thighs, up the sides of her waist, finally settling on her firm, hard nipples. He gave them both a gentle tweak.

Bridget needed no further encouragement; she began to ride the hard length of him. Every stroke was pure ecstasy against her sensitive flesh.

Her soft groans and sobs of pleasure were soon all that could be heard in the room.

※

Bridget lay sprawled on top of Stephen's chest on the chaise lounge. He had never been one for these pieces of furniture, often finding them too small for him. But this one was wider and longer than any other he had seen. Almost custom-built for a man of his physical stature.

After draining the last of the wine from his glass, he set it on the floor. He picked up the bottle and chuckled. It was empty. "We finished that in the blink of an eye."

He had brought her to completion twice now. The first time, she had ridden him. At the point when he'd sensed she was close to the edge, he had thrust hard and deep up into her, exalting when she cried out for more.

The second time had been a long, delicious encounter where Bridget lay over the mahogany leather sofa while Stephen took her firmly from behind.

With the wine gone, now came the time when a gentleman asked politely of a lady, "Are you finished with me for this evening? If you are, please say so, and I will take my leave."

She lifted her head and met his gaze. The cat who had got the cream couldn't look more satisfied. "I can still walk. And there is another bottle of wine waiting for us in my bedroom. So, Sir Stephen, I would say that your work is not yet done."

Brushing her hair from her face, he placed a soft kiss on her lips. "Well then, I believe we should adjourn to your private boudoir, Lady Bridget. There is nectar of the gods to be drunk and more sexual peaks for you to conquer."

Bridget rolled off Stephen and stood. He got to his feet

and gave her a wicked grin. Bridget squealed as he picked her up and slung her over his shoulder.

As he marched out into the hallway, Stephen prayed there weren't any servants lurking about. There would never be a good way to explain why the mistress of the house was draped face down over the back of a large, naked man.

Chapter Twenty-Four

Sunlight was streaming through the window when Stephen woke the following morning. For a moment he wasn't certain where he was, then it all came flooding back.

He was in Bridget's bed following the longest and greatest night of sexual pleasure he had ever known. Finally, he had found a woman who could hold her own against him in the passion stakes.

What a night. What a woman.

He stretched his arm out, seeking her body.

If I am lucky, we might get to enjoy another round of ecstasy before I leave.

Empty sheets greeted his searching fingers. He moved farther over in the bed. Perhaps she was someone who slept on the edge. Again, he found only cool, smooth cotton.

What the devil?

He sat up and looked around. He was alone. A glance to the other side of the bed revealed a bedside table. Upon it, propped against a small vase, was a white card with **Stephen** written in elegant, female handwriting.

With a frown now etched on his face, he picked up the card and turned it over.

. . .

You were sleeping so soundly I didn't want to wake you.
I have an appointment in the city this morning.
A footman will bring you breakfast if you ring the bedside bell.
Let yourself out when you are ready to leave. And please send me the final bill for your work. I shall recommend you to my friends if ever they are in need.
BD

Stephen was flabbergasted. A woman had got out of his bed before he had the chance to slip away. He wasn't going to quibble over the fact that the bed was actually hers. It was more that it had never happened to him before. Women didn't leave first—the man always did.

It's just not the done thing.

If Bridget intended to start conducting discrete liaisons, she was going to have to learn the rules. There was a set accord of acceptable behavior in these situations. Leaving a man sleeping in your bed was not one of them.

A chap might get to thinking he had been used purely for his sexual prowess.

"And then tossed aside," he muttered.

It simply wouldn't do. And the next time he spoke to Bridget he would set her straight.

Last night had not ended in accordance with the *ton's* unwritten book of bed etiquette. As a gentleman, it was up to him to ensure that the error was corrected. If he let it stand, then Bridget might get hold of the foolish notion that she could be the one in charge when it came to *affaires secretes*.

"I should insist on a repeat of the evening. That's what I should do."

He was an avowed rake, he owed it to Bridget to instruct her in the correct manner of how discreet sexual liaisons were conducted.

She will thank me for my selfless offer of private tuition.

With Bridget gone, there was no point in him lingering in bed. He was most certainly not going to ring for tea and toast, nor go and sit by himself in the dining room while *her* servants waited on him. A man had his pride.

Throwing his legs over the side of the bed, Stephen rose. He collected his scattered clothes and quickly dressed.

One of the few good points about never having employed a valet was that he was well-equipped to deal with the morning after a sexual encounter. By the time he left Bridget's house a mere twenty minutes later, Stephen looked the very picture of a well put together London gentleman.

On the surface, there was not a hair out of place. Inside, however, he was quietly steaming. He had years of no-strings-attached sexual liaisons under his belt. Love and leave them, was his unofficial motto.

Bridget Dyson had done exactly the same thing that he had done to countless numbers of women. A night of passion followed by a hasty departure. Just because the tables had been turned, it shouldn't bother him.

But it did.

She got up and left. Not even a good-morning kiss. And who leaves a note?

A woman remained in bed, pretended to be asleep, and let a gentleman slip quietly from her house. It saved both parties from stilted, awkward morning conversations.

His mind was made up. To ensure he did his duty as a gentleman, he would spend another night savoring the delights of Bridget's naked body while bringing her to sexual release. Then in the morning he would be the one to leave.

And if she still didn't grasp the rules, and arose before

him, he would return the next night. In fact, he was more than willing to continue to offer himself until she had been thoroughly educated.

Stephen licked his lips. "I hope she is a slow learner."

Chapter Twenty-Five

The rest of the day Stephen spent impatiently waiting to hear from Bridget. By late afternoon, he couldn't endure it any longer. His pride simply wouldn't stand for it. Out the front of the RR Coaching Company offices, he hailed a hack.

"Berkley Square and hurry," he ordered, climbing on board.

The cool reception he received from Bridget when he was ushered into her drawing room a short while later, did nothing to help soothe his wounded ego. If the way she smiled sweetly at him was any indication, there had been an obvious shift in the power base of their relationship, and Bridget damn well knew it.

"Hello, Stephen, I wasn't expecting to see you again so soon. Weren't you going to collect Toby from Harry and Alice's house today?"

He took in a deep, calming breath. "Alice has taken young Toby to visit with her parents. They are not expected home until late this evening," he replied.

It was hard enough dealing privately with the guilt he felt

over not spending enough time with his brother—explaining it to Bridget only made matters worse.

As cool as ice, she gently clasped her hands together. "That sounds delightful. Well then, you must be here to bring me your final bill. Case successfully closed and another client well satisfied." Her voice was heavy with innuendo.

She is good. Now what am I to do?

"I didn't come here with the intention of discussing money," he replied.

Having slept with a client before the financial side of things had been finalized made things beyond awkward. Not that he made a habit of involving himself in sexual relationships with his customers. The majority of his clients were men, so the situation rarely presented itself. He was sailing into uncharted waters.

How on earth am I ever going to ask her for money? I wish her brother was back in town. Then again, no I don't. He would start asking questions.

Questions which Stephen was in no mood to either entertain or answer. Besides, if Tristan Linton settled the account, he would have few valid reasons to call on the luscious widow. That wouldn't do. She was badly in need of his further instruction.

Bridget closed the distance between. A pair of sweet, teasing eyes met his. "If you didn't come for money, then what else could it be? Don't tell me you left a handkerchief behind."

Her sultry voice had his manhood standing stiffly to attention. As long as he lived, the memory of Bridget crying out his name as she climaxed wouldn't ever leave him. He swallowed deeply, struggling to maintain the last vestiges of his self-control. "You were gone when I woke this morning. I came to tell you that . . ."

Her fingers brushed against the front of his trousers, back and forth.

For heaven's sake, woman, take me in hand.

"Tell me what? That I was a naughty girl who should have ridden you again? You were sleeping so soundly, I reasoned I had tired you out."

Have mercy on me, woman.

"I have tickets for the opera for tonight. A private box. I thought you and I could spend an evening together," he replied.

Are you insane? Where did that come from?

Her hand settled on his crotch. "I love the opera. But that doesn't solve the problem of me owing you money. I don't want to feel like I am indebted to you. It might create expectations, especially in the back of your private box."

She squeezed his cock, and Stephen's breath grew ragged.

"If you come to the theater, then you won't owe me anything. The price of my final bill is your time," he replied.

And your fingers stroking me.

"Which opera are we going to see?" she asked.

I haven't the foggiest. It is going to take all afternoon just to find an opera box that is available.

To his relief and frustration, she released her hold on him. Mischief danced in her eyes. His gaze settled on her soft, pink lips. He would never get enough of them.

Stephen traced the tip of one finger across Bridget's collarbone before bending and placing a soft kiss on her skin. "Does it really matter?"

She flicked open the top button of his trousers and slipped a hand inside. Her fingers wrapped tightly around his erect manhood. "I suppose not."

Chapter Twenty-Six

Bridget was a fan of opera and had spent many an enjoyable evening listening to the wonderful music of such greats as Cavalli and Mozart. It didn't take long, however, for her to realize that Stephen didn't share her passion for the music.

The curtains had barely opened on the stage before his hand was on her knee. She kept her gaze fixed on the performers, while he slowly pulled up her skirt.

Stephen leaned over and whispered in Bridget's ear, "Have you ever had sex at the opera?"

Heat raced up her neck. The mere thought of it had her cheeks turning to flames.

"No. I have had moments of great emotional connection but not actually become aroused," she replied.

Please. Touch me. Do what you did with your tongue this afternoon.

Her gaze drifted from the stage to Stephen as he moved forward in his seat. He dropped to his knees on the floor, which considering his height and size was no small feat.

"Good, then that means I will be your first. And your most memorable."

A thrill of lust coursed down her spine as he gripped the sides of her skirts and bunched them up, settling them on her lap. Cool night air kissed her heated sex.

"No one can see you. Just me. Now spread your legs, Bridget. Let me sample that honey pot I have been dying to taste since the moment we arrived."

If she had thought to protest or to even say no, the words were beyond her. The second Stephen's tongue touched her folds, Bridget lay back and surrendered. Her fingers gripped the sides of the chair as he unleashed his masterful skills of oral pleasure upon her sensitive flesh. He licked, sucked, and then shockingly nipped at her bud with his teeth. Bridget closed her mouth as tightly as she could, desperate to stop a groan from escaping. The people in the next box must surely be able to hear.

The torture he inflicted on her sex was exquisite.

"Stephen," she whimpered.

He slipped one and then both of his thick thumbs into her. The stretch and slight burn was almost too much. Rising up on his knees, he began to stroke deep. "Tell me if you want me to stop. I want you to feel a little pain, but only if it is what you want. If it brings you to orgasm."

She had never experienced anything like this before. Never thought the line between pain and pleasure could be so razor-thin. Every time she thought she wanted him to release her, the aching demand to find her climax held her at his command.

"Tell me what you want," he said.

"I need. I need to come. Oh, Stephen, please, I want you inside me," she begged.

There was a flurry of movement, and the next thing he was settling her onto his hardened cock. He thrust hard and deep into her, and she sobbed.

"Stephen, yes."

The people in the opera box on the opposite side of the

theater would have a clear view of them, of what they were doing. She should be shamed by this behavior.

He speared his fingers into her hair. "Come for me, Bridget. Show your man what he means to you."

Their lips met as she finally crashed through into a blinding orgasm. He pumped furiously then let out a long groan of satisfaction as he followed her with his own climax.

Her head dropped onto his shoulder and he wrapped her up in his arms. The music continued, the song distant and unheard. Her ears were filled with the loud thump of her heart.

I think I am falling in love with you.

The words were on the tip of her tongue, but she dared not give them voice. She was already smitten with Stephen, a man who was determined that no woman would ever hold his heart.

Their relationship had already taken her to the dizziest of sexual heights, but the only way for her to escape was to fall. There was nothing Bridget could do, except brace for the inevitable impact.

Chapter Twenty-Seven

They didn't see out the rest of the opera performance. Within minutes of them both returning to earth and after adjusting their attire, Stephen called for an attendant to have their carriage brought around to the front of the theater.

As soon as they reached Bridget's home, it was a race to the bedroom and the beginning of a second, long night of passionate lovemaking.

Bridget couldn't remember how late or early it was when she finally fell asleep in Stephen's arms, but the sun was well up in the sky when she awoke.

He was gone.

She lay on her back staring at the ceiling, while her mind and heart battled one another for supremacy.

I love him. Don't be a fool. What if he feels the same as I do? This is Stephen Moore you are talking about; the man is a renowned rake.

Rolling over onto her side, she glanced at the door, praying that at any moment he would step through it and come back to bed. As the minutes ticked by, hope faded, and she eventually called for her maid.

There was no word from him that day, nor the next. When she finally summoned the courage to send him a note, she regretted having done so as soon as it had left the house.

Stephen had made his position clear; one night only. And if he had stuck to that, she might have been able to save her heart. But for her, he had broken his cardinal rule. He had spent two nights and one long afternoon in her bed. And there was the opera.

The longer she spent with him, the more times they made love, the deeper the hole she had dug for herself. She wanted him, but she wouldn't beg. He had to be in this alongside her. Never again would she be a fool and suffer the indignity of unrequited love.

A reply to her missive arrived mid-morning on the third day. It was short and painfully to the point.

Lady Dyson,
Sir Stephen is working with a new client and is at present unable to spare the time for social calls. I hope you understand.
A.T. Jones.
RR Coaching Company

"He can't spare the time for social calls," she muttered.

The sheer effrontery of the man. It was a good thing Stephen had declared he had no intention to ever marry.

"Because no sensible woman would have you. Fancy ending things in such a cold and perfunctory way."

A wave of sadness washed over her.

"He did say he couldn't promise you anything. And he never stayed for breakfast."

She screwed the note up and tossed it into the fire.

Relationships of any kind were always fraught with danger. She had learned a hard lesson in allowing herself to yet again succumb to the temptation of love.

It was time to put her heart back on ice and forget about Stephen. Hopefully, the memories of their lovemaking and falling asleep in his arms would fade, and he would become nothing more than a dim and distant name in her past.

"The next man I involve myself with had better stick to his hard and fast rules about dalliances."

Sir Stephen Moore had shared her bed for the very last time.

Chapter Twenty-Eight

T*hree weeks later*

As much as he tried, Stephen couldn't get Bridget out of his mind. His initial attempts at avoiding her had only stuck due to a pressing and dangerous case involving an old friend of the rogues of the road, Lisandro de Aguirre, the Duke of Tolosa and Maria de Elizondo, the kidnapped daughter of the Duke of Villabona. By the time Lisandro and Maria finally set sail from Portsmouth on the *Night Wind* bound for Spain, it was close to three weeks since Stephen had last seen Bridget.

It should have been plenty of time for him to get the sexy widow out of his system. To forget about the wonder of being with her, of sharing the most intimate of moments. But his every waking hour was spent thinking about her. And at night, she came to him in his dreams.

He was at a loss to explain the effect she had on him. He had never had this sort of problem with a lover before.

This is the price you pay for going back to the same bed more than once. Fool. I hope you have learned your lesson.

While Gus slept on the long ride back to London, Stephen spent hours staring out the window of their coach. If only he could get Bridget out of his mind. No woman had ever had this effect on him.

This is madness.

Stephen Moore never felt anything for anyone. He was a product of his uncaring parents. Aloof should have been his middle name. Yet, Bridget had somehow managed to crack his hard veneer.

As soon as they reached the RR Coaching Company offices in Gracechurch Street, Stephen hailed a hack. If he couldn't get her out of his system, then at least he could get into her bed. "Berkeley Square," he instructed the driver.

She greeted him, in her drawing room, arms crossed and stony faced. A horrible sense of foreboding settled in his mind. The last time he had been in this room, Bridget had been feisty and ready for more of his sweet loving. This time, however, to say that the air between them was frosty would have been a gross understatement.

"Sir Stephen," she said.

He had never had to grovel to a woman before and could now understand why men did all they could to avoid such situations. "I must apologize for my silence," he began.

Her gaze ran disapprovingly over him.

This is not going well. Damn.

When she didn't respond to his attempted apology, Stephen continued, "I had an important case to deal with and could not come to see you."

Bridget huffed. "You mean you didn't have time for social calls. I think that was the essence of the note which your friend sent. Sorry, if I cannot quote its contents verbatim, but I destroyed it."

Blast. I should have asked Gus what he put in the note.

Stephen had been too busy helping Lisandro at the time to actually pen the letter himself. He had assumed it would have made mention of him undertaking a perilous task. Something that Bridget would hopefully understand.

"I am sorry if Gus didn't put things as eloquently as I had hoped. I couldn't come to see you, and I am sorry. We only arrived back in London from Portsmouth a short while ago, and I came straight here," he replied.

She shook her head. "The fact that you couldn't be bothered taking the time to pen the note yourself speaks volumes for what you really think of me. I shouldn't, of course, be surprised. I've seen the way you treat Toby. People are not a priority in your life, Stephen. And that includes those who should be able to expect emotional commitment on your part."

This was going from bad to worse.

"I said I was sorry." Even as the words rolled off his tongue, a sinking sensation settled in his gut. Bridget wasn't the least bit interested in hearing his apology.

She pointed to the door. "Please leave."

"What?"

"I thought you and I had the beginnings of something. A spark. The past three weeks have shown me the folly of my hopes. You are not the first man to make me feel a fool over love, but in your case, I don't have to wait until you die to move on with my life. Get out, Stephen, or else I shall have the servants toss you into the street."

Anger born of humiliation flared within him. "This is the exact reason why I don't get involved with women. You are too emotional, always wanting more than a man is prepared to give."

Bridget crossed the floor and opened the door. "This is your last chance to leave in a dignified manner, Sir Stephen."

He stepped toward the exit, stopping when he reached her side. His jaw was set hard as he glared down at her. A better man would not seek to intimidate a woman in such a way, but with his blood pounding behind his ears, Stephen wasn't capable of clear thought. "You will come crawling back to me. And when *you* are ready to say you were wrong, I might consider hearing your apology."

The door was slammed hard and loud behind him as he stomped off in the direction of the stairs. "You'll be begging me to see you again—I know you will," he grumbled.

Chapter Twenty-Nine

F*our weeks later*

Bridget lifted her head from where it hung over the chamber pot then thought the better of it. On her hands and knees in the middle of her bedroom, she cast up what had to be the last of the contents of her stomach.

She had no idea what was causing her to feel so wretched, but this was the fourth morning in a row where she had found herself on the floor within the first few minutes of rising. The previous day's bout of violent vomiting had seen her go back to bed and spend the rest of the day under the blankets fast asleep.

This morning, however, she had a modiste's appointment with one of London's most in-demand dressmakers. She couldn't afford to miss it. If she did, it would be weeks before she could secure another booking.

When the last of the heaving finally subsided, she sat back on her haunches. Sweat dampened her brow.

"At least it seems to pass later in the day," she muttered.

As soon as she returned home from her dress fitting, she would send for her personal physician. A tonic to settle her stomach was no doubt all that she required.

Her current state couldn't possibly be due to anything other than her having eaten bad food.

※

"This is ridiculous. Are you certain you didn't cut the bust a size too small?" said Bridget.

The seamstress frowned. "Lady Dyson, I have been making your gowns since you were a girl of eighteen. Your measurements have never changed."

Bridget was standing on a raised dais in the salon of her modiste later that morning, being fitted for her new aqua and white floral gown. A gown which appeared destined not to cover her breasts properly.

"Exactly, which means that one of your girls must have accidentally cut the bust line to the wrong size," Bridget replied.

She ignored the *tsk* and indignant huff from the dressmaker.

People make mistakes. I am not seeking to blame anyone; I just want the gown to fit.

Like a mother hen pecking around the barnyard, the modiste scurried off, returning a moment later with a measuring tape in hand. A young woman followed closely behind.

"I checked the notes for Lady Dyson's fittings. The fabric was cut exactly to the same measurements as always," protested the girl.

Bridget stood silent. Not only did she not wish to become involved in any argument, but she was still struggling with the aftermath of this morning's bout of nausea and vomiting.

When the modiste slipped the measuring tape around Bridget's back and drew the ends together tightly over her bust, she held her breath.

Please don't let me cast up my accounts in the dressmakers. I would never live it down.

The woman leaned in close, peering through her spectacles to read the numbers on the tape measure. "Hm," she murmured. She adjusted the tape before taking a second reading. "Polly, my dear, would you please go into the storeroom and start packing away the new bolts of silk which arrived this morning?"

The girl gave Bridget a brief glance before curtsying and leaving the room.

As soon as the dressmaker's assistant had left, the modiste turned to Bridget. "Lady Dyson, you have always been strict on your eating and maintenance of your figure. Have you perhaps been eating a little more of late? Indulging in even the odd extra tea cake or bun can make a difference."

Bridget sighed. "No. In fact, I have been ill every morning for the past few days. I have barely kept any food down. By rights, I should be swimming in my gowns."

The modiste met her gaze. "Would you allow me to touch your breasts?"

It was an odd request, but Bridget was intrigued. "If you must."

She pulled the top of the badly fitting gown down, leaving only her silk chemise covering her breasts. The modiste lay a hand over Bridget's left breast and gently squeezed.

Bridget instantly flinched.

"Is it tender to my touch?" asked the woman.

Bridget nodded. "Very. My breasts have been particularly sensitive over the past few weeks. I plan to see my doctor later today."

The modiste looked away, giving a pensive "hmm".

"What is wrong?" said Bridget.

"This is all rather awkward, considering that you are a widow. Rest assured, Lady Dyson, that because of your marital status, I am choosing my words with great care. When was the last time you had your courses?"

A cold chill settled over Bridget.

I can't be.

Her pulse began to race. When had she last bled?

Today was the first day of December. She counted out the weeks on her fingers. November, no. October, no. All the way back to mid-September. The last time she'd had her courses was shortly before the incident with the blackmailer.

Right before she had met Sir Stephen Moore.

But it was impossible. She was unable to have children. The doctors had said so. Rupert had made certain that all of London society knew his wife was the *Barren Baroness.*

She put a hand to her chest as tears broke free. "How can this be?"

"Well . . ."

"No. I know how it happens, but I was married for four years and never fell pregnant with my husband's child."

The gown suddenly felt uncomfortably tight. She fought to get out of it as a rising tide of panic gripped her.

"I need to leave. I must go home," she stammered.

The modiste reached out and took a hold of her arm. "Your husband has been gone for over a year. But obviously another gentleman has caught your eye. Let me promise you that my discretion is absolute. If a miracle has indeed occurred, Lady Dyson, you won't be the first client whom I have made home visits to over the years in order to keep such a matter private. Just send word and in the note mention that you have injured your leg and are unable to travel to fittings. I won't send any of my girls, rather I shall handle this personally."

Bridget swallowed deeply. Gowns were the last of her concerns. If she was indeed pregnant, it was Stephen's baby.

A man with a well-deserved reputation for avoiding personal commitment.

I am a widow. And if I am with child, I am in deep trouble.

She had just narrowly averted a shocking scandal. Was she about to leap into another even greater one?

Chapter Thirty

"A boy. A dog. A..."

Stephen leaned over and pointed at the word Toby was struggling to pronounce.

"This one has one more letter than the others, but you just have to slow down and try. What is the first letter?"

"F," replied Toby.

"Very good. Now the next one is 'R'. So, what do you have?"

A bright smile lit up Toby's face and he clapped with glee. "Frog! A boy. A dog. A frog."

Stephen patted him gently on the back. "Well done."

Toby's reading was improving every day. Mostly due to Alice's efforts, but Stephen was also taking the time to spend at least an hour every day helping his younger brother with his studies. The big, old, battered dining table in the offices of the RR Coaching Company was the perfect place for them to sit and work.

He cast a friendly eye over the boy as Toby turned the page and started on the next words. It had only been a matter of months since the young lad had come to live at Gracechurch Street, but in that time, he had made himself very much a part of the place.

Even gruff Andrew McNeal, the Duke of Monsale, had taken a shine to Toby. Earlier that morning he had arrived bearing a basket of berries and plums freshly picked from his garden just for the boy. Stephen's heart had swelled with pride as his young charge counted them out on the table before helping himself to a hearty serving.

The question of what he was going to do with his brother in the long term was yet to be established. The current arrangement of Toby spending most of his time, and nights, at Harry and Alice's house was not something that could be maintained forever.

Nor was the situation with regard to Toby's name and status. The boy would eventually start to ask questions, and even if he didn't, then strangers likely would. The question as to why Stephen had brought a stray orphan back to London with him would be topmost in people's minds.

Admitting their familial connection was oddly something Stephen was reluctant to do. As long as he remained simply Toby's guardian, their relationship would exist merely as friends. He feared the changes and expectations that would come once his brother knew the truth.

I don't want him to know because then he will want me to not only help take care of him, but to show him brotherly affection.

With that sort of fondness, Toby would no doubt come to love him. And love was something Stephen had no idea how to handle. Or give.

˚

The Steele family carriage came and collected Toby at exactly three o'clock every afternoon. With the recently married George Hawkins no longer helping Gus with his cross-channel smuggling trips on the *Night Wind*, it had fallen to Stephen to undertake the task. Small boys could not be left alone at night. And despite Toby's protests, nor could they be taken all the way to France.

When the knock came at the door of the offices, Stephen assumed it was because his young charge had, as usual, left something behind and one of Harry and Alice's footmen was waiting outside to collect it. He was still wracking his brains as to what Toby had forgotten when he opened the door and found not a Steele-house footman but rather a Dyson footman standing on the threshold.

The man bowed and offered Stephen a note. "Lady Dyson instructed me to deliver this to you."

Stephen went to close the door, but the footman put a boot in the way. "She was specific with her instructions. You are to read the letter and then come with me back to Berkley Square."

So, she has finally decided that it might be in her best interests to apologize. I'm not sure if I am still interested in her or not. That boat may have already sailed.

He ushered the footman inside. "Give me a moment to read this, and I shall get my coat. Help yourself to the pot of coffee on the table. It should still be hot."

With letter in hand, Stephen headed to the privacy of his room. He had an inkling that it would be best if he opened and absorbed the contents of the note on his own.

He broke the seal and unfolded the paper.

Dearest Stephen,
I need to urgently speak with you. It is a delicate matter and not one I wish to share with anyone else at present.
My carriage will bring you to my home.
Bridget

"Cryptic. Hmm. Please don't let her mother have gone and done something foolish. I don't think I could handle another Linton family case."

Considering how their last encounter had ended—the one where she had thrown him out of her house—he felt well within his rights to refuse. And if it was indeed a delicate matter, she was hardly going to come knocking on his door if he did.

He sighed. It might have been weeks since he had seen her, but Bridget had got well and truly under his skin. He couldn't refuse her.

"Mores the pity."

Her remarks about him not giving a damn for other people had stung. They still did. He should just send the footman away and go back to trying to forget about Bridget.

And how has that been working out for you? Or are you going to continue to pretend that you don't think about her a hundred times a day? Or that you search for signs of her at each and every party you attend.

He wasn't going to even consider the fact that in the many weeks since he had last shared Bridget's bed, he hadn't been with any other woman. None of the wicked wives of the *ton* tempted him.

"Oh well, at least she is the one who has yielded. It's not my carriage sitting out the front of her house while a footman is delivering a note begging for an audience."

Picking up his coat, he stuffed the note into the pocket. He headed back into the main room, where the footman was draining the last of a cup of coffee.

"Let's go. I would hate to keep Lady Dyson waiting," said Stephen.

He would come at her summons, but he was determined that she would be the one offering up the first apology.

Minx. Took your sweet time, but you clearly want more of me.

Chapter Thirty-One

Bridget was standing in very much the same spot in the upstairs drawing room that she had been in when Stephen last saw her. But this time instead of her arms being folded across her chest, they hung in front, her hands clasped tightly together. He couldn't recall having ever seen her look so ill at ease.

And pale.

All his thoughts of gloating and making her beg for forgiveness fled his mind. He hurried over to her. "You are not well. Have you seen a physician?"

She gave a halting laugh. "I am feeling better today than I have in a long time. And in answer to your question, yes, I have seen a doctor. In fact, that is why you are here."

Huh?

"Please have a seat. What I have to say may come as a bit of a shock, so you should be sitting down. I know it certainly floored me," she said.

Stephen took a spot on one of the sofas. His nerves tingled when Bridget came and sat beside him. He wanted to reach out and take a hold of her hand, but her stiff posture stopped him.

I've missed you.

Any thoughts of them rekindling their affair dimmed as he took in her nervous fidgeting. The tight smile on her lips added further to his growing discomfort.

"I don't have to explain the wonders of nature to you or . . . oh." She wrung her hands. "Sorry, this is harder than even I had imagined it would be."

Ignoring the warning bells which were going off in his head, he settled his warm hand over hers. "Just start at the beginning and be as clear as you can. I wouldn't bother with the metaphors."

"Alright. Have you ever heard of male infertility?"

Stephen raised an eyebrow. This was most certainly not the topic he expected to be discussing. "I have heard of men not being able to perform sexually."

Not that it had ever been a problem for him.

"Yes, well I have discovered that a man can 'get it up' and still not be able to sire any offspring. I don't suppose it is something that men even consider a possibility. If no children are produced in a marriage, the woman bears the blame."

Stephen raised his free hand, slipping a finger into the top of his cravat. It was suddenly too tight.

"It would appear that my late husband suffered from this condition; and by connection, so did I."

Bridget took a hold of his hand and raised it to her lips. For a moment Stephen was in two minds as to her motive for this sudden display of affection. Was she offering comfort or trying to prevent him from fleeing?

Her grip tightened. "Stephen, I am pregnant. With your child."

Chapter Thirty-Two

❦

Fatherhood...

Stephen had once had a rope break from under him while scaling down the side of a castle in France during the war. The fall to the ground, while not a long one, had still left him with serious bruises and a sore back. It had taken many weeks for him to recuperate.

But there was no way of ever recovering from what Bridget had just said. This was life altering. He was dumbstruck.

The only saving grace was the fact that he was still in possession of his faculties, and therefore not foolish enough to inquire as to whether she was sure it was his child.

"Would you like a whisky?" she asked.

He shook his head. While he could cheerfully have murdered a glass or three, alcohol was not the solution to his problem. The problem of what to say to Bridget.

"Now I know this has probably come as a bit of a shock to you," she said.

Understatement of the year.

"Yes. Of course, if I had known that the issue lay with

your husband, I would never have put you at such risk," he replied.

Bridget's fingers slipped away. He turned as she shifted on the sofa, creating a definite space between them.

"Forgive me. I don't expect that was the first words you wished to hear from my lips after receiving your news," he said.

She got to her feet. "Should you want nothing to do with either me or our child, then please say so. If that is the case, I shall make my own arrangements to deal with the situation going forward."

He finally summoned up the courage to meet her gaze. "This child will have my name. As to the rest of it, I don't honestly know. Marriage was never in my plans."

"Nor mine," she bit back.

That hurt. He could dish out rejection but had never been good at receiving it.

Stephen rose from the sofa and came to Bridget's side. "Just give me a little time to absorb the shock. We will marry, and I shall organize to have suitable financial settlements made. There will be no scandal, and you will be protected."

He would give her a wedding and ensure that their child was legitimate. The urge to pull Bridget into his arms, kiss her, and make further promises battled with his hardened heart. He didn't know how to offer comfort or affection. Honesty was his only true weapon.

Bridget closed her eyes and nodded. "Have your solicitor send over the paperwork as soon as possible."

"Bridget, I . . ." he stammered.

She pointed toward the door. "I am not surprised. Disappointed, of course, but you are nothing if not true to form. You can see yourself out."

Stephen bowed then silently left the room. It was only when he was outside and headed for Gracechurch Street that the reality of what he had just done finally sunk in.

That was cold, callous, and uncaring of me. I am just like my father.

Chapter Thirty-Three

It could have been worse. He could have refused to marry her. Dealing with an illegitimate child brought with it all manner of social and legal problems. She would likely have had to retire permanently to the country. At least this baby would now have its father's name.

"And you will have the child which you longed for all these years," she muttered.

She would also have Toby. Stephen had been quite taken aback at her demand for the young boy to come and live with her, but Bridget was determined that he should have a proper home. No child deserved to be living in the dusty, poorly furnished rooms of a coaching company.

And he needs a mother.

If Stephen wanted nothing to do with them, so be it. She would raise their little family in the manner she saw fit. Without the interference of her standoffish husband.

I shall survive. Stephen will take over the lease on this house, and he will give me money. Our sham of a union won't be any different to that of many other ton marriages.

She had already dealt with one cruel and heartless husband; another one couldn't pose too much of a problem.

And Stephen, for all his faults, wasn't Rupert. He would do the decent and honorable thing.

And he won't go around London society telling everyone what a dreadful wife I am and that I haven't furnished him with an heir.

Her words of self-assurance echoed hollow in her mind. She had fallen for the tall, rugged rogue; her heart had broken long before she discovered her unexpected pregnancy.

But he had made his position clear. And while the pain of it burned deep, she couldn't fault his candor.

Bridget rubbed her hand over her tiny baby bump and blinked away the tears. She had a child growing inside her—a baby she would care for and love all her life.

"I won't have you growing up without a loving family. If that family has to be you, me, and Toby, then we will make the best of what we can," she whispered.

If Stephen decided he wanted no part of their lives, that was his loss.

But does he understand the magic and joy he will be missing?

Chapter Thirty-Four

After several letters had been exchanged via their respective solicitors, the marriage settlements between Sir Stephen Moore and Lady Bridget Dyson were close to being finalized. Three days prior to their wedding, and only a few minor points were still outstanding, one of which included the times when he was expected to visit Berkley Square and see his child.

His continual wrestling with the problem saw Stephen seeking the wise counsel of his fellow rogues of the road as they gathered around the grand table in the RR Coaching Company office early one afternoon.

"I have taken some time to think about this marriage business," he began.

The recently happily wed George Hawkins frowned. "Such a romantic. I already pity your future wife."

Stephen ignored the comment. He had suffered enough of them from his friends since announcing his betrothal and future marital arrangements. No one appeared in favor of his plans. Even Monsale, the man renown for being allergic to weddings, didn't hold back on his obvious contempt.

"You are a fool," muttered Monsale.

"That may be, but I am a fool with a plan." Stephen lay a long piece of paper out on the table and began to read. "Days to visit. Sunday from quarter past the hour of ten until quarter to the next hour. Christmas Eve and Good Friday, a full hour."

The others exchanged glances. Gus and Monsale both frowned.

George glared at him. "Utterly ridiculous. Next you will be offering up various saint's days."

Gus clapped his hands together. "Saint Anthony of Padua. Patron saint of lost people and women seeking husbands."

Harry snorted. "No, he needs Saint Marinus. Patron saint of comic actors, jesters, and those suffering afflictions of the mind. Because you have to be either in jest or touched in the head to think Lady Bridget is going to let you get away with that. My ears are still burning from hearing Alice's reaction to your absurd plans to never live under the same roof as your wife."

George nodded his agreement. "Jane, my blushing bride, said some very choice words when I told her that your marriage was going to be in name only. Suffice to say you won't be welcome at Coal Yard Lane any time soon."

Stephen screwed up the paper and tossed it in the general direction of the fireplace. He didn't bother to check if it made it into the flames. "What am I to do? She has demanded that Toby come and live with her. If I visit, I have to make an appointment. You make it sound like this is all of my making. And she refuses to take my name."

Monsale, who had been leaning against the table at the far end, righted himself. He cleared his throat and the room fell silent, waiting on his pronouncement. "Stephen, my poor deluded friend, I might well be doing my best to hold cupid at bay, but even I am not that blind to your predicament. The chit holds your heart, and she isn't planning to give it up any time soon. Give in—the battle is lost."

Pushing back his chair, Stephen got to his feet. He had heard enough. "I made a vow many years ago that I would never marry. Circumstances now see me having to go through with a wedding. She gets the protection of my name, nothing more. Well, the child does at least."

Harry sighed. "You don't know what you are missing. I would have thought your upbringing would see you crave the love and joy of a family."

Stephen moved toward the door. "Bridget knew what I was when we became lovers. And what I was offering. Nothing has changed. As for love, I don't even know what the word means."

His friends were right in many ways, the most obvious being that he was a fool. Bridget may well hold his heart, but Stephen had no idea how to unlock the chains that kept it bound.

He had backed himself into a corner, and stubborn pride would keep him there.

Chapter Thirty-Five

Bridget's second wedding was in sharp contrast to her first. There was no glittering service at Saint Paul's cathedral, nor was there a grand ball with hundreds of people. Her brother and parents were not in attendance.

If Stephen was determined to have but a façade of a marriage, she was most certainly not going to inflict it on her family. She had written to her father explaining the situation and assured him that a trip to London would be a waste.

The only guest Bridget could truly claim as being hers was Lady Naomi Steele. And even then, she was the sister of one of Stephen's closest friends.

In the end all that really mattered to her on this day, was that the child growing within her belly would be guaranteed to legally have its father's name. In time, she would deal with the rest.

Lady Bridget Dyson and Sir Stephen Moore were married quietly at her home in front of a small gathering of friends. And Toby.

She had held firm in her determination that the young boy should come and live under her roof. By marrying Stephen, she was now Toby's sister-in-law. He would be the baby's uncle once it arrived. Whether her new husband liked it or not, she was building a family. Their family.

As Stephen slipped the wedding ring onto her finger, he leaned in and brushed a soft kiss on her cheek. "You look lovely, Bridget. Positively glowing."

"Thank you."

She wasn't going to give him any more than scant polite conversation. His last-minute request to store some of his personal things at her house had been refused.

You can't have it both ways, Stephen.

He was either fully invested in them and a future together or he was going to be kept at arm's length. There was no middle ground when it came to her heart.

Steeling herself for the congratulations of their guests, Bridget went to give her regards to the Duke of Monsale.

Monsale greeted her with a friendly hug, and she accepted his felicitations. "Well, you have managed to get the first battle of this campaign under your belt. You are now Lady Moore. What I am interested in, however, is what your strategy is for winning the war?"

Andrew McNeal was a strange man. Most of her encounters with him had left Bridget with the distinct impression of a cool, aloof creature. Someone whose past had reputedly included time held captive by pirates and whose path to the dukedom had been cleared by the sudden and mysterious deaths of both his uncle and father.

But there were times when she caught glimpses of a softer side. He seemed to have a kind regard for Toby and a magical ability to produce sweets and small toys from out of the depths of his coat pocket whenever the boy was in his presence.

"My new husband has made his position clear. This child was a problem that required a solution. With this marriage, he has dealt with it. It's just like all the other cases he handles. Results guaranteed," she replied.

Monsale's brows furrowed. "I have known that fool for many years. And I also understand the damage that his upbringing has done. Believe me, I know what it is to have terrible parents. But there is something I don't think either of you have realized."

The sound of raised voices had Bridget's gaze settling on her spouse. Stephen was in conversation with Gus Jones and, even from this distance, it was obvious via the shouting and wild hand waving that they were having a spirited argument.

"What's going on with the two of them?" she asked.

Monsale shook his head. "Mister Jones is headed to France on the late tide tomorrow evening, he is leaving for Portsmouth within the hour. Stephen wants him to delay the trip a day or two, so he can accompany him. Since it is your wedding night and all, Stephen says he is obliged to be with you tonight. But back to the topic of our conversation."

She tore her attention away from her husband. "You were saying we don't realize something. What do you mean?"

"Stephen is in love with you. It's as clear as the nose on his face, which is not in any regard small. And it doesn't take a quizzing glass to see that you are obviously smitten with him. I am of the firm belief that it is going to take but a little time and a steady hand for you to break down the walls that fool has built around his heart."

Bridget fought to keep her composure. It would be wonderful if the reality of their situation was as Monsale claimed. If her hopes and dreams could come true. "How am I to get him to see the truth of his heart? I don't think he even knows he has one," she replied.

"He does, and it's not a bad one either. I've seen him with Toby. He cares for the boy. He could have easily left his father's bastard hidden at the family estate or even ignored the lad. Instead, he put him on his horse and brought him to London. Did you know that Stephen sits with his brother most nights and talks to him until Toby falls asleep?"

"No, I didn't."

And with Toby now residing under her roof, Stephen would no longer be able to share that tender moment.

Monsale gave a gentle squeeze of Bridget's hand. "Sometimes you have to teach love to people. And that might include being tough with their emotions. Send Stephen to France. Deny him his wedding night. Make him realize that poor choices have consequences."

She hadn't been looking forward to later this evening. To the inevitable showdown over where Stephen would sleep tonight. He wasn't going to like hearing what she intended to inform him regarding that particular matter.

If I don't have you, you don't get me.

"What if I push him away and he doesn't come back?" she replied.

"Well, then he is a bigger fool than any of us. Trust yourself on this, Bridget. If there is any man in this room in greater need of a loving family than Stephen Moore, I haven't seen him." Monsale bowed. "Just remember my words. Please excuse me, Lady Moore, I must go and have a quick word with Lady Naomi before I leave. She will take grave offense if I don't."

Bridget stood alone for a moment taking in the room—the small gathering of guests, the odd uncomfortable glance in her direction.

Her hand settled over her belly.

Forgive me if I fail. I won't condemn you to a life of forever hoping your father might come to care for you, to show you his love. He will be your Papa in every way, or he will be a stranger.

It was a gamble. The biggest of her life. Bridget could only hope that it paid off.

With her back straight and her mind made up, she headed toward Stephen and Gus. Her new husband would be spending his wedding night on the road, and she would be at home praying for a miracle.

Chapter Thirty-Six

"Bloody stubborn woman and her ridiculous demands."

Fancy expecting him to live under the same roof as her and raise a family. Hadn't he made his position on the subject clear enough? The marriage settlements were in black and white. Even the details of where Toby would live had been covered by the lawyers.

Nothing, however, had prepared him for this sudden change of plans. Bridget had pulled the veritable rug out from under him.

She sent me away. I didn't even get a wedding night.

Stephen lifted the bottle of whisky to his lips and took a long drink. He was alone up on the weather deck of the *Night Wind*, watching as the English shore disappeared into the darkness. He had barely been a husband for a full day, and his marriage was already effectively in name only.

His arm dropped, and the bottle fell onto the deck with a large thud. He didn't bother attempting to pick it up, rather he sat and stared as the whisky flowed out and over the side of the yacht.

"I should have stayed and demanded my conjugal rights," he muttered.

He was angry and frustrated. And to make matters worse, even in his half-drunken state, there was only one person whom he could blame. Himself.

Bridget wanted a real marriage—to have their baby born into a functioning family. And she was set on demanding that he played his part.

What even is that?

His only experience of family was that of a twisted caricature, something that if you stared long and hard enough at it, you could just discern the outline of a blood connection. Nothing more.

"I thought I might find you up here, drowning your sorrows."

Stephen lifted his gaze in the direction of the voice. Gus stood, hands on hips, staring at him. A look of great disappointment sat on his face.

"If you have come to judge me, you can sod off. I wasn't the one who forced me to sail with you. You should take that up with my wife," replied Stephen.

Gus dropped beside him and picked up the empty bottle. He shook his head.

"I thought you gave things enough of a nudge last night in the coach on the road to Moore Manor. Let that be your last drink until after we have got the shipment of brandy and are headed home from France." There was an edge to Gus's words, one which Stephen didn't like. He sensed something was wrong.

Stephen narrowed his eyes. "Are you expecting trouble?"

The rogues of the road didn't lie to one another when it came to matters of life and death. It was a firm policy to which they all stuck.

"Possibly. There is a new gang operating out of Lamballe a few miles inland from the coast. Former French soldiers who, according to our friend Armand La Roche, have a number of the local authorities in their service. They are led by a man named Vincent Marec, and from what I hear, he is not to be underestimated. I am not sure how many more of these trips I am going to be able to undertake. I haven't told any of you this before, but the last trip wasn't without incident," replied Gus.

Stephen sobered up somewhat at hearing this news. "Why didn't you tell us?"

Gus shrugged. "Harry and George have both been busy with their wives, Monsale his estate. And you seemed distracted after your father's death. I figured a woman must be involved somewhere, and I was privately hoping you might have finally found love."

Stephen stared hard at the deck; regretting having spilled the last of the whisky. This sort of conversation was difficult no matter what sort of state of sobriety he was in. Being drunk, however, would have made it a little easier.

I just wish I wasn't feeling anything.

"You think I am wasting the opportunity that having Bridget in my life presents. Monsale has said much the same, though not in such polite terms."

Gus chuckled. The Duke of Monsale was well known for his foul-mouthed, but still eloquent speeches. He was not one for mincing his words.

"I could tell you that how you live your life is none of my business. But then again, what sort of friend would I be if I did that? An important part of our long friendship has always been that we speak plainly with one another."

"So, you are going to add to the chorus of opinion?" replied Stephen.

"No. I am going to ask you one question. I don't want you to give me your answer—I just want you think. When we get back to London, you should go and talk to Bridget. She is the one who needs to hear your considered response, not me."

Well-meaning friends were the worst. They were also

exactly what Stephen needed. He had been stubbornly pushing people away, refusing their counsel.

And look where that has got you.

Stephen sighed, there was no point in delaying. "Alright, so what is the question?"

"You and Bridget have a connection. When the two of you were engaged in your affair, you were walking around like a love-struck fool. You didn't see it, but we did. So, now that you have this woman as your wife and she is carrying your child, why on earth are you finding reasons to avoid her?"

Gus got to his feet and headed farther along the deck. He stopped to talk to the yacht's captain, leaving Stephen alone with his thoughts.

Because I am in love with her, and I haven't the foggiest notion as to how I am supposed to live that life. Or even if I am worthy.

Chapter Thirty-Seven

Stephen woke alone and cold on deck a little after dawn the following morning. Someone had thrown a blanket over him during the night, but it had done little to keep the chill wind of the English Channel out. The scant sleep he had managed to get did nothing to improve his mood from the previous night. He had been a fool in walking away from Bridget on their wedding day.

Wiping the sleep from his eyes, he struggled to his feet.

The mouth of the river Gouët loomed into view. Soon enough they would be at Château-de-La-Roche and meeting up with Armand and Evangeline to secure the shipment of brandy. By nightfall, the *Night Wind* would be on its way back to England.

But every hour that Stephen was away from his wife, now seemed like a year.

"I should never have got on board this bloody boat," he grumbled.

He turned as Gus, resplendent in his usual smugglers disguise of tricorne hat, long black wig, and greatcoat, made his way up from below deck. The sight of two coffee cups in his hands was most welcome. "I came to check on you a few hours ago, but you were swearing in your sleep, so I left you to it."

Stephen accepted the offered hot drink and took a sip. *Heaven.* A strong mug of coffee was the only thing which stood a chance of making him feel more human this morning.

"How are you feeling? Did your time up here give you the opportunity to contemplate the error of your ways?" asked Gus.

Stephen stared at his cup. "Yes, it did. My only regret is that I am here and not waking beside my wife. I should have stood my ground when she insisted on me going with you."

Gus gave him a hard but friendly slap on the arm. "Good to hear. Now go and throw some fresh water on your face. I want to be in and away from the jetty below the château as quickly as possible. I would like very much for us to avoid any encounters with Marec and the Lamballe crew today."

By the time Stephen had finished his coffee, the *Night Wind* had sailed into the mouth of the Gouët river, passing under the watchful eye of the medieval Tower of Cesson. The tower, which was now in ruins, had stood for over four hundred years, guarding the entrance to the waterway that led to the town of Saint-Brieuc on the coast of Brittany.

Gus's smuggling associates, the Le Roche family, owned Château-de-La-Roche, which was situated not far up the river and well away from the port authorities.

Stephen normally enjoyed this part of the trip. The sight and smell of France always brought back fond memories of the time he had spent here in his youth. Today, however, he just wanted to reach the château, help with the crates of brandy, and then leave.

The ship's crew were gathered on the weather deck, while Gus and Captain Grey finalized their instructions.

"If you don't need to leave the ship, then stay at the dock. Unfortunately, we will not have time for any of you to visit the town, or the taverns," said the Captain.

Groans of disappointment arose from several members of the crew.

There will be some very unhappy French mademoiselles in Saint-Brieuc tonight. Sorry, chaps.

Gus held up his hand. "I know we often stay the night and sail for home with the morning tide, but circumstances have changed. And as much as I would like to see each and every one of you sharing the bed of a pretty and welcoming lady of your choosing, we cannot stay."

The grumbles continued for a moment. To his credit, Gus let the crew voice their annoyance. When the men fell silent once more, he continued, "Sir Stephen will oversee the loading of the brandy onto the ship, while I manage the transport of the crates from the château. Let us work quickly and with care. We have new enemies, and they mean business."

While the crew set about readying the yacht for docking, Stephen pulled Gus to one side. "Are you sure you don't want me to come to the château with you? Another pistol might be worthwhile having."

Gus gave a quick glance around, then leaned in close. "I don't want a gun fight. If we can get in and out without those limp pricks from Lamballe knowing about it, I would be more than satisfied."

His friend was clearly not telling him the whole story, but now was not the right time to challenge Gus over the truth. Stephen had a job to do and that was to protect the boat and the shipment. Once they were safely on their way back to England, then he would have a quiet word with his fellow rogue of the road.

A welcoming party was waiting for them as the *Night Wind* drew up alongside the small jetty below the bluff on which Château-de-La-Roche sat. Stephen and Gus each gave a friendly wave to Armand La Roche. When a second figure stepped out onto the wooden pier, the smile on Gus's lips died. "Damn," he muttered.

Evangeline La Roche stood beside her uncle; a long shotgun draped across her arm. Bridget might well think herself handy with a pistol, but Stephen had seen the French noblewoman in action. She was a deadly aim.

Pity the fool who went up against her in a gun fight.

"What's wrong?" he asked.

Gus sighed. "If Evangeline is carrying a loaded weapon, it means that there has been more trouble. We might have just sailed into a large problem. One we may not be able to easily handle."

At the dock they were greeted by a worried looking Armand. "I am glad but not pleased to see you, my friends. The Lamballe scoundrels have been causing more strife. We might have to do a short load this trip and then get you away as fast as possible."

"Marec's men have been seen in the woods nearby this morning. You shouldn't have come, it's too dangerous," Evangeline said more bluntly.

Stephen observed the silent argument that quickly took place between Evangeline and Gus, at the end of which she gave a resigned huff. "Well, you are here now. Your trip shouldn't go to waste. Let's get this done."

While Gus followed the La Roche's up the steep hill toward the château, Stephen checked his weapons. Taking up a vantage point on the deck, he scanned the horizon for any sign of unexpected and unwelcome visitors.

The first cart full of crates of French brandy arrived shortly after. As the crew hurried to offload them, Stephen kept his gaze on the small thicket of trees at the top of the hill. If they were going to come under attack, that would be the likely direction from which their assailants would approach.

They were a good third of the way into unloading the

second stack of crates an hour or so later, when the sound of gunshots rang through the air. A dust cloud appeared at the top of the rise. There was shouting and more gunfire.

And then a deathly silence.

The crew all stopped what they were doing and every single one of them turned to Stephen. He caught the expression on their faces and the look in their eyes. Fear. Uncertainty. Silent pleas for someone to step in and save them.

He cocked his rifle. "Forget about the rest of the brandy—get on board the yacht!"

Crates splintered and glass shattered as the contraband was quickly abandoned. Heavy footsteps rattled on the gangplank. Captain Grey bellowed orders to make ready to sail.

Stephen's attention and rifle were now firmly focused on the road. As the sound of an approaching horse reached his ears, he settled over the gun sights.

A tall, slim rider with long brown hair trailing in the breeze rode into sight.

Evangeline.

She didn't spare her mount, riding at breakneck speed down the slope. When she finally reached the jetty and pulled hard on the reins, Stephen's blood turned to ice. Behind her on the horse, head slumped against Evangeline's back, was Gus.

"He has been shot!" she cried.

Stephen handed his rifle to the nearest crewman and dashed along the gangplank. Reaching the horse, he managed to catch Gus as he toppled and fell.

"We were ambushed," said Gus. The dark patch of red on the front of his shirt had Stephen swallowing down a bout of nausea. He had never been great with blood but seeing it on his friend made it doubly worse.

"You have to get Augustus to a doctor in England, and I must go back and find my uncle. We have to fight the Lamballe gang, or we will never be rid of them."

Evangeline dug her heels into the side of the horse, and it kicked away.

Stephen wrapped an arm around Gus and helped him to the boat. "Come on. Let's get you on board. The quicker we are away the sooner someone can take a look at your wound."

Gus winced and offered a tight smile. "I don't expect it will be you doing any surgery. Or at least I hope not."

By the time they had Gus on board the yacht and had taken him below, Captain Grey and the crew had set out every possible sail. There was only a small gust of wind blowing as the boat slowly, tortuously slid away from the jetty.

Pistol drawn, Stephen raced back up to the weather deck, coming to stand alongside the other members of the crew who had their weapons trained on the shore. His heart pounded in his chest, adrenaline coursing through his every vein. If the Lamballe gang tried to attack a second time, they were going to be met with deadly force.

Try it and see how many bullets I will put in every one of you blackguards.

Seconds passed by agonizingly slow, but eventually, they were far enough away from the shore to be out of pistol range. It was clear that the new rival gang of French smugglers had decided that their message had been well and truly delivered.

This is now our territory. Stay away or die.

"Stand down," he ordered the crew.

Stephen headed for the ladder and the lower deck. His heart still thumped hard in his chest; adrenaline now replaced by fear. In the hot, cramped space, the air was rank with the metallic smell of blood.

Captain Grey and another crew member were huddled over Gus who lay on the floor. As Stephen approached, he was struck by the almost deafening lack of noise. No one spoke. Gus didn't make a sound.

He stopped, blinking back sudden tears. He may not have wept or grieved much over the passing of his father, but if Gus was dead, this loss would come as a body blow.

The captain lifted his head and met Stephen's gaze. "He has a bullet lodged in his chest. It's bad but hopefully not fatal. As soon as we make land in England, we need to get Mister Jones to a doctor."

"Stephen," croaked Gus.

Summoning his courage, he came to Gus's side. The significant amount of blood on both the smuggler's shirt and the cloth which the captain held over the wound had Stephen swallowing bile.

"Sorry about this, Stephen. Deuce foolish of me to go and get shot."

The rogues of the road had always treated serious injuries with a stupid amount of levity. Monsale had made them all solemnly promise that if they died during a job, they would go with a grin on their lips.

Seeing Gus so badly injured sorely tested Stephen's humor. No one would be laughing if his friend didn't survive the journey home—least of all Monsale.

"Does it hurt?" he asked.

"Only when I breathe," replied Gus.

Stephen screwed his eyes closed and nodded. "Well, you are going to have to put up with the pain because I won't stand for you to bloody well die on me. I've already got more than enough to deal with when I get home."

"I wouldn't want to add to your problems. And it would be the height of bad manners for me to perish while you are technically on your honeymoon. I don't think your good lady wife would be too pleased."

Stephen's thoughts turned to Bridget. She would be beside herself with worry if she could see where her husband and his friend were right this minute.

What am I going to tell her when I get home?

Another crewman appeared in their midst. "We have reached the end of the river, and the English Channel is in sight." The man handed Captain Grey a small brown bottle. "It's all we have, but hopefully, it will make Mister Jones comfortable."

Gus eyed the bottle and grimaced. "The joy of opium. Do what you have to with this bullet wound, and then let me have the laudanum. Stephen, I think this is where you take your leave and go up on deck. I expect there is going to be plenty more blood and a spot of screaming on my part, so off you go."

Stephen met his friend's gaze and nodded. "Alright. I will come and sit with you later." He headed for the ladder.

Please lord don't let him die.

Chapter Thirty-Eight

The wind and tide were against them most of the way, making the crossing of the Channel a slow and difficult one. Stephen sat staring at the French coastline as it faded into the distance. If Gus survived the night, changes were going to have to be made, the whole French smuggling operation carefully examined and reassessed.

So many things were now coming to an end. They had been running illegal goods between England and the continent for some three years now. Before the end of the war and Napoleon's fall, the trade had been quite lucrative. But with Europe now at peace, they were having to deal with the threat of former French soldiers seeking to make money in the smuggling game.

"It's just getting too dangerous," he muttered.

Gus stirred in his cot and cracked open a sleepy eye at him. "Yes, it is. I had hoped I might be able to get a few more shiploads of cargo handled before I had to call stumps. This mess is my fault. I misjudged our rivals and how violently they would defend what they now claim to be theirs."

Stephen gave him a rueful grin. "Promise me you won't

ever go back to Saint-Brieuc. Otherwise, I may just have to burn your boat."

Gus sighed. "If I do it won't be for a long time. I doubt my mother will let me leave the house for the next six months."

Rightly so.

"The laudanum is wearing off, but I don't want any more of it. Once we make it to Portsmouth, I need to be able to walk ashore. If anyone sees me being carried off this boat, they are going to start asking questions."

"If we can get you to Moore Manor, then Granville should be able to find a doctor to attend you," replied Stephen.

"No. No country doctors. We press on for London," replied Gus.

Gus's determination to travel while still in such pain made no sense. It only added to Stephen's growing concern. "What are you not telling me? And if you think to concoct a lie, don't bother. Because if you do, I will take you straight to the nearest surgeon in Portsmouth as soon as we dock."

Gus grumbled something foul under his breath. "It's not just France where things are getting dangerous for the smuggling game. Last month, I was almost caught by the customs militia in England. To say it was a close thing would be kind."

One by one, the rogues of the road were having to face the reality of a changing world. With both Harry and George now moving away from the illegal side of the business, it was time they looked at other options.

"So, you, like the rest of us, are going to have to come up with some other career choices. Ones which don't involve either getting shot or hung," replied Stephen.

Gus clutched at his chest and let out a long painful groan. "That hurts like the devil."

"Monsale, of course, won't like it, but he is not going to be able to say much otherwise. Harry and I both have wives who are expecting, and it wouldn't surprise me in the least if George follows suit very soon."

Babies and new business ventures would have to wait. That was the future, and in the meantime, they were going to have to deal with the more immediate and pressing issue of what to do with the badly injured Gus.

If he couldn't get Gus medical attention before they reached London, it was imperative that he did so as soon as they arrived. He needed somewhere to hide his friend. And just as importantly someone who had experience in dealing with gunshot wounds.

Stephen scrubbed at his face with his hands. "Bridget is going to kill me."

Chapter Thirty-Nine

"They will surely put you in Bedlam asylum after this," muttered Gus.

Stephen couldn't argue with his friend's opinion. Only a madman would bring a badly wounded smuggler to the house where his new bride lived. A house where he himself wasn't exactly welcome.

It was late at night by the time they finally made it back to town the day after they reached Portsmouth. While Gus snatched whatever sleep he could, Stephen had stayed awake, wracking his brains as to other places they could go.

The searching of his mind whilst sitting in coaches and carriages was becoming somewhat of an unwelcome habit.

After arriving via the rear mews of the house at 12 Berkeley Square, he and the driver managed to get Gus out of the coach. It took several minutes for the injured rogue to be able to stand upright. Stephen told the driver to wait.

"I will be out as soon as I can. I have a pregnant wife to deal with before then."

"Bridget is a practical woman—she will understand," said Gus.

I hope so, otherwise this is going to be ugly.

The first piece of good fortune he had encountered in some time came in the form of the Dyson household head butler and a footman. They both happened to be outside having a smoke when Stephen and Gus started for the door. They threw their cheroots to the ground and hurried over.

When the butler didn't bat an eyelid at the sight of Gus, Stephen recalled Bridget's remark about her former husband having hunting accidents regularly covered up.

The butler nodded to the footman. "Go and inform Lady Dyson, I mean Lady Moore, that her husband has returned home and has a friend seeking peace and quiet."

Stephen gave a nod. "Thank you."

Clearly peace and quiet was Dyson household code for 'find the mistress and tell her someone has been shot.'

As the footman headed inside, the butler addressed Gus. "Are you in need of a physician?"

Gus sighed. "No, I was attended to on the boat. I just need a bath and then a bed. Sleep would be wonderful"

"Very good, sir."

As they stepped toward the door, Stephen glanced back over his shoulder and caught the man's eye. He whispered, "Bandages and laudanum."

They were met by Bridget in the hallway. She was clad in a dressing gown, with slippers on her feet, her rumpled hair evidence of her having already been in bed.

His wife gave Stephen the merest of chin tips in greeting, focusing her interest on Gus instead. He couldn't blame her. Few people would take kindly to having a wounded smuggler arrive on their doorstep in the middle of the night.

She took one look at Gus and frowned. "Let's get you upstairs. We don't want the rest of the servants seeing you in this state."

It took the combined efforts of Stephen and the footman to help Gus climb the stairs to his room. Gus winced, complained, and groaned the whole way. Once inside the first of the spare bedrooms, he rallied. "Just put me in the chair by the fire."

Stephen shook his head. His friend needed rest and pressure to be taken off his wound. "The bed is the best place for you. We can't have you bleeding again. You have already lost enough blood."

The butler appeared bearing a tray with several large rolled up bandages and a bottle of laudanum large enough to put an elephant out of its misery. Bridget quickly dismissed the two servants. "Thank you. Now both of you head downstairs. And not a word."

As soon as they were gone, she closed and locked the bedroom door. When she reached the bedside, Stephen caught his first real look at her. She looked tired and pale. He had a horrible suspicion that being pregnant wasn't the only cause for her less than sparkling countenance.

"What happened?" she asked.

"Nothing. I slipped on the weather deck of the yacht," said Gus.

Stephen sighed. There was no point in lying to his wife. The moment she saw the wound she would know it had been caused by a bullet. "He was ambushed on the road leading up to the château where we get our illicit brandy supplies. There is a new rival group operating out of a nearby town. Our friend, Armand, warned us about them, but I think even he underestimated their veracity. It took quite an effort to get the *Night Wind* safely out to sea."

"I wondered why you were back so soon. You weren't meant to return until late the day after tomorrow," she said. "Not that I am complaining in seeing you again."

He took her words to heart. Bridget had not only made special note of when he was due home, but she appeared at least a little happy to see him.

"Clearly this new gang is dangerous. Something which

you are all going to have to take into account in future," she said.

"Yes. We will have to address the question of future trips to France among the rest of the RR Coaching Company directors. As for myself, that was my last voyage. I have a wife and family to consider," he replied.

"Do you?" Her voice broke on the words.

"Yes. Have no doubt as to where my priorities now lay. They are with you, Toby, and our baby."

Gus let out a pained gasp. From the extent of his injuries, it was clear it was going to take quite some time for him to recover. Time in which he hopefully would be convinced that his days of running contraband were well and truly over.

With Gus stretched out on the bed, Stephen motioned for Bridget to walk farther away. Once they were closer to the door, he bent and whispered, "We had the bullet removed and Gus stitched up onboard the boat, but he refuses to see a doctor. I know you mentioned having experience with the hunting wounds of Rupert and his friends, so I was hoping . . ."

"Of course, that's why we have such a large bottle of laudanum and an extensive selection of bandages. Let me have a look at him and see what I can do. If the wound has been kept clean and stitched properly, he will basically just need lots of bed rest. But if it is not in a good condition, we may need a physician."

"No doctors," cried Gus.

Stephen rolled his eyes. "Let Bridget have a look at you, then we can decide. I'm not having you die under my wife's roof just because you are a stubborn ass."

"Our roof," she corrected him.

He caught a hold of her wrist. "I am serious about my priorities, of what is now the most important thing in my life. Please, Bridget, can we talk? I mean, have an honest conversation about us; one which results in there being an agreement about our future."

Bridget nodded. "After I have changed Gus's bandages and doped him up with opiates."

A relieved Stephen released his hand. His wife appeared far too comfortable with the notion of having a badly injured man under her care.

Yes, well you haven't bothered to find out much about her. Or what life was like with that heartless first husband of hers.

Not that he had started off her second marriage any better.

The way he had treated Bridget was the same as he had done with all the other women in his past—bed and forget them. Or in her case, he had tried to get her out of his mind.

But he was determined that things with her would be different, starting the minute he got back from Monsale House. He had to inform the group's leader of the events of the past few days. "How angry with me will you be if I leave Gus in your care for a short time and go to see Monsale?"

Bridget headed toward the bed where, after unbuttoning Gus's greatcoat, she peeled open his torn shirt exposing the bandages. To Stephen's relief, no blood had seeped through them.

"Just go and then hurry back. He is not the first semi-naked man I have seen in my life," she replied.

Stephen halted in his progress to the door.

"I swear on the cross of Saint Nicholas that I am incapable of any form of lechery in my current state," said Gus.

Stephen pointed a finger at his wife. "Just don't let him try and sweet-talk you. That man has been known to convince women to make terrible errors of judgement."

He opened the door and was halfway through it when he caught Bridget's reply.

"When it comes making foolish mistakes, I think it might be a little too late for that, Stephen."

He kept going. The sooner he spoke to Monsale, the quicker he could be back. And when he returned, Stephen was going to set his wife straight. The fool in their relationship had always been him.

But no more. He was going to become the husband she needed him to be and the man who deserved her love.

Chapter Forty

The top bandages came off relatively easily. The ones which pressed against Gus's skin, however, posed a more difficult challenge. They required the use of a pair of scissors and the patient gripping the bedclothes tight.

"You do know that the large lump loves you?" said Gus through gritted teeth.

Bridget pulled the last of the dressings away and stared at the angry wound. It was dry but at some point, it had bled through the stitches.

"Not with any degree of certainty. This is Stephen we are talking about. A man who has never known love and struggles with the mere concept of it," she replied.

Gus placed his hand over hers and gave a squeeze. "You hurt him when you sent him away to France. And I don't just mean his pride over the wedding night. He missed you."

Over the past couple of days, Bridget had pondered whether she had been wise to push Stephen away. While she had taken Monsale's counsel on board, the final decision had been hers.

The idea that Stephen might be finally coming around to dealing with the truth of his feelings for her had Bridget fighting back tears. "Yes, well he is not the only one who has been in pain. I don't think either of you considered my feelings when you sent that perfunctory note about him not being able to make social calls. That really hurt."

Gus winced. "The note was my fault."

She met his gaze. "But the abandonment was his. If Stephen is going to make any effort at a marriage and family, he has to understand that you don't just walk away from people. And when you are with them, you cannot hold them at arm's length."

This was the conversation she should be having with her husband, not his friend. Still, it was good to actually give voice to the thoughts and emotions which had been running almost constantly through her mind since that horrid day. Even now, long weeks after she'd berated Stephen for his lack of care, the hurt had not fully subsided.

I'm going to continue punishing him forever if I don't give him a chance.

"Stephen has asked for us to talk once he returns. We shall see what he has to say." She reached for a soft, wet flannel from the bowl beside the bed before dabbing at the dry scabs around the wound. "Hush now. I have to concentrate while I clean the stitches."

And I need time to think.

Picking your battles was one of the realities of marriage. The outcome of tonight could very well dictate the rest of her and Stephen's future.

The only fight Bridget wanted to win was the one for their family.

Chapter Forty-One

The six-storied, Portland stone Monsale House loomed large over Mount Street. It was taller than every other mansion in the neighborhood. Even the impressive Duke of Strathmore's house on nearby Park Lane came up ten feet short.

But the house itself paled into insignificance against the stature of its owner. Andrew McNeal, fifteenth Duke of Monsale, was standing hands on hips in front of one of the massive fireplaces in the grand ballroom when Stephen arrived. About the floor were scattered various pots and plants. A half-empty shipping crate was to one side of the door.

Monsale pointed to it. "Just arrived from Morocco this morning. Some of the rose bushes didn't survive the sea voyage. I am most disappointed."

Stephen stifled a grin. Monsale became a different man when he was talking about his beloved roses. His sharp edges dulled. The other members of the rogues of the road knew well to inquire about his precious petals before they gifted him with any sort of unpleasant news.

"Sorry about the flowers," replied Stephen.

Monsale stirred from gazing lovingly at his floral children and fixed him with a hard stare. "Why are you here? I thought you went to sulk in France."

"We were ambushed in the woods just below the château. Gus took a bullet in his upper chest."

The color drained from the duke's face. "Where is he?"

"At Bridget's house. We removed the bullet onboard the *Night Wind,* but he won't seek professional medical attention. Bridget is changing his bandages. Apparently, her late husband had a habit of shooting his friends while out hunting," replied Stephen.

A trail of violent curses followed Monsale as he headed for the door. It was all Stephen could do to get out of the way as he stormed past and into the foyer.

"Get the coach and the palanquin!" he bellowed.

There came a muffled reply, then more swearing from Monsale.

"The blasted litter. You know the stretcher for carrying people."

He returned to the ballroom. "Why didn't you bring Gus here straight away? Your poor, much put upon bride should not be having to deal with this. Do I need to remind you that you are a bloody fool?"

Stephen gritted his teeth. Now was not the time to lose his temper. "You always said that we were never to bring trouble to your door. And besides that, Bridget didn't complain. Gus is fine where he is."

A hard slap to the back of the head was Stephen's reward for his impertinence.

"She must really love you to put up with such nonsense. Either that or she is wishing that you were the one shot."

Stephen had already heard more than enough, and now his head hurt. "Enjoy your roses, Monsale. I have an errand to run at Gracechurch Street, then I am going home to my wife."

I have delivered the news, and my task is done. There are more important things to worry about.

He made for the door, but stopped, and turned back to his friend. "You are right. I am a bloody fool. And if you ever hear me again refer to my home as Bridget's house you can slap me twice."

Chapter Forty-Two

An hour later, Stephen returned to the house on Berkeley Square. He marched upstairs carrying a large box. Two footmen bearing his travel trunk followed. At the top, he nodded in the direction of Bridget's bedroom.

"Put it in there, thank you."

He went in search of his wife. It was time for them to talk.

He spied a light shining through the open door of the main drawing room and headed toward it. Bridget was seated by the fire, her hands resting in her lap. She rose as Stephen stepped into the room.

"How is Gus?" he asked.

"Gone."

He halted mid-stride, stunned. Gus had been fine when he had left to go and see Monsale. What on earth had happened? "What? How?"

She smiled. "Monsale came and took him. Had a group of his servants carry Gus out on a litter. It's a pity you missed the whole spectacle—it was rather amusing. Gus looked for all the world like Queen Cleopatra as they carried him downstairs. Though I don't expect that she complained as much as he did when she was being borne about."

"You had me worried there for a moment," he replied.

That explains the need for a palanquin.

"Monsale grumbled about you being a dolt for bringing Gus here. I did protest on your behalf. Explained that I had experience in handling hunting wounds, but he wasn't having any of it. Said you and I had more important things to concern ourselves with," she added.

Monsale was right. At least with Gus gone from the house, he and Bridget would be free to talk—to share the evening without the worry of constantly checking on their patient.

Bridget approached, then stopped. Stephen hated himself for having made her feel she couldn't come to him without hesitation.

I want to see the open arms of my wife when I come home.

He took a slow, measured step toward her. And then another. When he finally stood before his wife, Stephen sucked in a shaky breath. He glanced at the box. "I expect you are wondering what this is and what I have to say."

Tears shone in her eyes as she silently nodded.

"Come and look."

Bridget followed as Stephen carried the box over to a nearby table and set it down. After pulling a key out of his pocket, he unlocked the box and lifted the lid. Inside were various bundles of banknotes, gold coins, and precious jewels. "This is my flee box. Each of the five of us has kept one over the years. It contains what we would need if we ever had to make a run from the law."

"And that is why it is called a flee box?" replied Bridget.

"Exactly. We built a strongroom under the stables at Gracechurch Street, and the remaining boxes are still stored there. Since Harry and George have both married and given up the criminal life, they have withdrawn their boxes."

Bridget slipped her hand into his. "And so, have you."

Not a question, a simple statement. It gave Stephen hope.

"I also brought my travel trunk here tonight. I want you to

know that everything I own and hold dear is now under this roof. Our home."

With his retirement from illicit work, Stephen no longer had the need for secret funds to escape from England.

"You said home?" she replied.

"Yes, home." He reached into the box and took out a small black bag. It had sat unopened and forgotten for many years. "The rattle that Toby's mother gave him is the only memento he has of her. This is all I have of my mine."

He handed her the bag, but instead of opening it, Bridget scowled. "Why are you giving me this? I don't understand what is happening. Please, Stephen, you have to explain."

"My mother left me and returned to her family in Scotland when I was barely six months old. I never saw her again. She died some ten years later; and I only discovered she had passed away by mere chance. Not one letter. She couldn't even grace me with a simple missive in all those years. It was as if I had never existed."

Bridget untied the bag and opened it. Inside was a small silver pin of a fox.

"I wore it for a time when I was younger. It was my talisman, the faint hope that she might come and take me home with her. My father used to mock me, so I took to wearing it on the inside of my jacket."

Raking his fingers through his hair, he took a deep sigh.

"I want more than just a trinket to be the sum total of our family. Bridget, I am here tonight to beg you to accept me as I am, faults and all. I want us to be a real family. You. Me. Toby. And our baby."

I want to come home.

Chapter Forty-Three

Bridget stared at the tiny silver fox. It was more than likely part of the crest from his mother's family. A family Stephen had never known.

He was a grown man, but the pain of a lifetime of rejection hung heavy in his words. Stephen had finally, hopefully, seen sense and decided that a life with her was worth living.

But she wasn't going to yield that easily. He was not the only one who had suffered from having their love thrown back at them—from being rejected.

"And you think because you suddenly decide that you want a family that I should just accept your decision? Because it takes more than just saying 'that's mine' for it to become true."

She could blame her emotions on the baby growing inside her. On the sudden and quite overwhelming mood swings she had been experiencing. But this was more than just a pregnancy thing. A shy, tentative smile appeared on his face.

"Well, I am your husband," he offered.

Bridget shook her head. "But not a very good one. Believe me, I have had more than enough experience to be able to claim authoritative knowledge of what constitutes a terrible spouse. If you can't bring all that you are with you to this home, Stephen, and I mean more than just your things, you don't deserve to be here."

Please. Please. Step up and be the man I need. I have so much love to give you.

"You have my all. And that includes my love. I love you, Bridget." There was rapture on his face as Stephen spoke the word which had eluded him for a lifetime. Love.

And then he smiled. She swore it stretched a mile. He brushed a hand on her cheek. Through a glassy haze of tears, she met his gaze. Tears shone in his eyes.

Oh, sweet lord, he is crying too.

"I mean it. I love you, Lady Bridget Moore. My wife. My heart. I will do everything I can from this day forward to be worthy of your love."

She sniffled. "What makes you think I love you? You are nothing but a rogue. How could any sensible woman fall for a man such as you?"

Stephen laid a hand on his wife's pregnant belly and whispered, "Because when it comes to me, you can't resist. You never could." He drew her into his arms. "Say you will give me a chance to be worthy of your love. I will never take it for granted."

"My love for you is precious. I am trusting you to keep it safe."

He lowered his lips to hers, sealing their pact with a tender kiss. Held safe in her husband's embrace, Bridget exalted. She had won. Her rogue was finally hers.

I am never letting you go.

Chapter Forty-Four

"Have a seat," said Stephen.

Toby took one look at the plate of biscuits the housekeeper had laid out on a nearby table and quickly snatched one up. With oat goodie in hand, he took his usual spot on the comfy green-and-white floral sofa.

The hard leather couch and chaise lounge had been moved to another private room, which only Stephen and Bridget used. The main drawing room had been freshly painted in a softer green palette and repurposed as the family room.

Stephen turned from where he had been staring out the window and considered the young boy. In the months since he had come to London and been in the care of first Alice and now Bridget, Toby had blossomed. The shy lad who had hidden behind the skirts of Mrs. Granville was long gone. In his place was a bright, confident boy.

"I wanted to talk to you about my father," said Stephen.

"Yes."

"Do you remember much about him? I mean, from when you lived at the house in Witley."

Toby bit off a big chunk of biscuit and chewed on it for a

minute. His expression was one of careful thought. "He was nice to me sometimes. But mostly he just told me to stay away. I don't know if he liked me much."

Stephen gritted his teeth. Even in his later years, his father —their father, couldn't find it in his heart to show affection to a small boy.

Cold, callous bastard.

"I don't think Sir Robert liked anyone. It wasn't in his nature," said Stephen.

Toby screwed up his face, and Stephen silently chastised himself.

Of course, the boy doesn't understand what you mean. He is six years old.

"I mean, it wasn't your fault he wasn't nice to you. He was the same with me when I was little. I spent many years in the kitchen at Moore Manor."

"Anyway. What I want to talk to you about is . . . you and me."

It was harder than he had imagined it would be to finally tell Toby the truth of his sire. Bridget had been right; he should have done it as soon as he brought the boy into his care.

Even now, it was a struggle to think of his brother as being more than a boy, a lad, or a responsibility. But he owned it to his family to try.

He strolled over from the window and took a seat next to Toby on the sofa. Keeping his distance from people he cared about had to be a thing of the past, of that he was determined.

"You see, my father was your father," said Stephen.

There was silence for a time; and he could almost imagine how those words might be rolling around in Toby's brain while he tried to make sense of them.

"Which makes you my little brother," he added.

Toby's mouth opened in surprise. His head turned and he met Stephen's gaze. A look of wonderment sat on his face.

And then his big, beautiful smile stretched from ear to ear.

Stephen wiped away a tear. Emotion welled up inside him. All those long, lonely years he'd secretly wished for a sibling, and now this little boy had come into his life and made his dreams come true.

He lifted Toby onto his lap. "And that also makes me your big brother," he said, giving him a tickle.

Toby squirmed and giggled in the way only small children do—honestly and from the heart. "Harry says you are a big lump, so that makes you my big lump of a brother."

Trust Harry Steele to be putting those ideas into young minds. He would be having a word with his friend about not corrupting his younger sibling. "Well, I don't know about the lump bit, but yes, we are brothers you and me. And we will stick together forever. Master Toby Moore, I am so very happy that you have come to live with Bridget and me. And that we are now a family."

Toby placed his small hand in the middle of Stephen's palm. "The night Sir Robert died, they brought me to his room. When it was just him and me, he said that a big man would visit soon, and he would become my family."

Stephen swallowed a large lump of emotion. Any moment now he was going to turn into a watering pot and cry a river.

Toby lifted his head and met Stephen's gaze. "And he was right. You did come for me, and now we are a family."

Stephen wrapped Toby up in his arms and let the tears fall.

Chapter Forty-Five

※※※

A *month later*

Lady Bridget Moore would never tire of the lustful, hungry look on her husband's face whenever he arrived home and discovered her lounging naked in their private sitting room. Nor did she ever protest at what always followed. Life at their home with Stephen was never dull.

And it was their home. With the income from Stephen's estate and the proceeds of his flee box, they were officially the owners of number 12 Berkeley Square.

At the sound of footsteps in the hall, she hurried over to the chaise lounge. By the time the door opened, she had thrown off her silk dressing gown and was reclining in naked splendor, waiting.

"One of these days it is going to be a servant who finds you in such a compromising position, Lady Moore," said Stephen.

Her maid had informed Bridget that the rest of the household had put two and two together and deduced the reason for the extra coal deliveries. The room was kept very warm during the evening. And with the servants aware that private encounters went on in this room, not one of them was going to be foolish enough to come knocking on the door.

Bridget draped her arm over the back of the couch, allowing him a full view of her breasts. They were plump and rounded—one of the many benefits that being pregnant had bestowed on her.

Stephen's gaze settled on her peaked buds, and he licked his lips.

"So how is Gus?" she asked.

The smuggler might have only been her patient for a few hours, but she was always wishing to hear news of his recovery.

Stephen stirred from quietly ogling his wife. "Bored. But other than that, he is fine. Recovering well. And if the number of nautical books he is currently reading is any indication, getting ready to set sail again soon."

You could take the sailor out of the sea, but not the sea out of the sailor.

He crossed the floor and came to kneel before her. "Enough talk of other people. I am far more interested in you."

Bridget gently ruffled Stephen's hair. "And how was your day? I was expecting you home hours ago. Toby was disappointed he missed you before he left to spend the night at my parents."

Grandma and Grandpa Bee were always keen to see Toby. Lord and Lady Linton had unofficially adopted Toby as their grandchild. He had taken to calling Bridget, Bee, so the name had been given to the rest of her family. Tristan found being called Uncle Bee highly amusing.

"I had a busy day. Our new coach arrived this morning, and I spent several hours interviewing possible drivers. After that, I had an appointment at Rundell, Bridge & Co, then went over to Monsale House to see Gus, and finally home," he replied.

She narrowed her eyes at him. What business did he have with Rundell, Bridge & Co, one of London's foremost jewelers? "I thought you had sold all the jewels in the flee box."

"I had, but after I set up Toby's trust account, there was some money left over. So, I decided to have this made."

Stephen produced a wide, flat blue velvet box from under his arm, and Bridget's heart began to race.

"I didn't do things right when we agreed to marry. In fact, I made a hash of things."

Bridget had forgiven Stephen for many things, but it was clear that he was still taking himself to task over the beginning of their marriage.

He offered her the box. "This is my way of setting things in stone. Pardon the pun."

With trembling fingers, she lifted the lid, and gasped.

"Oh, Stephen," she whispered.

Before her lay a full parure: a brooch, a ring, two bracelets, a pair of earrings, and a necklace that took her breath away—all were pale blue aquamarine, set in silver.

"I couldn't decide between the sapphires and these stones, but then I thought that the aquamarines better matched your eyes. Whenever you wear them, I can be reminded of what it is like to look into those blue pools of heaven when we are alone."

A flush of heat coursed through her body. She knew what he meant. When they made love, there was always that one glorious moment when Stephen stared deep into her eyes right before he brought her to climax.

"They are absolutely beautiful. I don't know what to say, other than thank you."

He lifted the necklace from the box and placing it around her neck, secured the clasp. The precious stones settled between her breasts.

"You don't have to say anything, other than the three words I always want to hear."

Bridget chuckled. "My fallen rogue?"

When he moved in for a kiss, she impishly nipped at his bottom lip. He growled. His eyes sparkled with mischief. It was fun to tease Stephen, to draw out the playful side of him. Until now, she doubted he even knew that part of himself existed.

"Do I get a special reward if I say them?"

Stephen set the jewelry box to one side. After placing his hands on Bridget's knees, he pushed them apart. "Yes, and more than once tonight."

She leaned forward and met his gaze. "I love you."

Epilogue

Andrew McNeal, the Duke of Monsale was a strange mix of a man. He had no qualms about handling what was known in the London crime world as *wet work*, yet he was fastidious about his garden. The lush greenery of the grounds of Monsale House were the talk of all of high society. Or rather they would be if Monsale ever let anyone other than his small tight-knit group of friends actually visit.

Gus Jones had been a guest at the house, recuperating from his gunshot wound for the past month, and in that time, he had not seen anyone visit the place other than the members of the RR Coaching Company. Even the wives of the rogues of the road were not offered an invitation to come for tea.

Someday however, Monsale would have to let a female into his secret sanctuary. A duke with a title and property, was in need of an heir.

It was the dead of winter, and the rose bushes lining the stone path which ran from the house to the rear high brick wall had been trimmed back to almost nothing. The rest of the garden beds lay sleeping under their blankets of straw, protected from the winter chill.

But the hot house where Monsale grew his treasured Moroccan roses was a riot of color. It was here that Gus spent most of his days, sitting quietly, reading, and making notes. This morning was no different. With a warm blanket covering his legs and a cup of tea on a nearby table, he was quite comfortable.

When the glass door of the greenhouse opened, he raised his head from the book on coastal tides he had been studying. Monsale's steward, Adan, approached him, bearing a tray.

It's too early for my midday meal. Though I could do with a spot of elevenses. But Adan never brings me food.

To his disappointment, the tray only held a small folded up note.

"This came for you a short time ago, Mister Jones," said Adan.

Gus took the letter and quickly examined it. The corners were creased and there were a number of grubby marks on the front. Dirty fingerprints told the tale of the note having passed through many pairs of hands before finally reaching him.

"Thank you," he said.

He turned the letter over, and the image of a griffin on the seal had him quickly dismissing Monsale's steward.

It's from Château-de-La-Roche. Please don't let it be bad news.

Gus cracked the seal and unfolded the paper. In his mind, he quickly translated the French in which it had originally been written.

Dear Augustus,

If you are reading this letter, then you are not dead.

Things have gone from bad to worse since you left.

> *My uncle has gathered a large store of weapons at the château.*
>
> *He means to go to war with the Lamballe gang and will not listen to me.*
>
> *Please do not return to Saint-Brieuc—it is no longer safe.*
>
> *Evangeline*

This was the worst possible news. Armand La Roche was a gentleman farmer not a warrior. The villains he was intending to go up against were all battle-hardened former soldiers. Men who had seen years of tough fighting under Napoleon.

"He doesn't stand a chance."

Gus glanced at the blanket which covered his knees. His wound was mostly healed, with only muscle tenderness still giving him any real trouble.

The truth was, he had remained at Monsale House because he couldn't think of anything better to do. He had steadfastly refused Stephen's repeated pleas for them to discuss the future of the smuggling operation. Even Monsale's efforts had been rebuffed.

Who knew that a duke could pout when he didn't get his own way?

Just because the rest of the rogues of the road were one by one retiring from a life of crime, didn't mean he had to follow suit.

"Besides, what else would I do?"

Peeling the blanket off, he got to his feet. He read Evangeline's note once more and made a decision. "I can't just sit here and smell the bloody roses."

It was time he went home, made his apologies to his parents for his shoddy treatment of them, and packed. He had heard the siren call. His friends needed him. The *Night Wind* would once more sail to France.

Augustus Trajan Jones was going to war.

Read Gus and Evangeline's story in
The Rogue and the Jewel.

In the burning, shattered ruins of a French château, smuggler Augustus Jones makes a promise to a dying man. He will find the men who have abducted his missing niece no matter what the cost.

But Evangeline La Roche is not a captive, instead she is on the hunt for revenge, determined that those who have sought to destroy her family will pay dearly for their crimes.

The last thing Evangeline needs is for Gus to appear and attempt to become her hero. While she has long held a secret attraction for the smooth talking Englishman, she has also made a vow to never trust a member of the criminal Rogues of the Road.

Bound by his promise, a reluctant Gus, is forced to go along with Evangeline's plan and sets out with her on the long road to Paris. Travelling through the wilds of Brittany, the first flames of desire spark between them. Both are powerless to resist temptation.

As they close in on their enemies, Gus and Evangeline are shocked to discover that the tables have suddenly turned, and they are now the prey. They face a desperate and dangerous race back to the coast to where a boat is waiting to take them to safety.

But will Gus be able to convince Evangeline that what they share is enough for her to flee her beloved country and start a new life with him in England?

Turn the page to read the first chapter of
The Rogue and the Jewel.

The Rogue and the Jewel

"Where is my pistol? I had it just a minute ago."

It couldn't have disappeared. Gus Jones frantically stuffed his hand into the pocket of his jacket, searching for the weapon, sighing with relief when his fingers touched cool metal. The gun was right where he had left it.

You dolt. How many times a day do you have to check for it?

Another anxious moment which had set his heart racing. The need to constantly have a loaded pistol close at hand was an odd response for someone who had so recently been shot.

There couldn't be many safer places than his family's home in London. In addition to that was the fact that the man who had tried to kill him was over two hundred miles away in France. But even the deep blue waters of the English Channel couldn't separate Gus from the painful memories of that day at Château-de-La-Roche, when a bullet had very nearly ended his life.

I am home, and I am safe.

These panic attacks made no sense; then again, they never had. The mind was a strange beast. You could tell yourself all the sensible things in the world but fear always lurked in dark recesses.

"You must focus on the task at hand," he chided himself.

Seated on the dusty floor of the cramped attic, he was taking an inventory of his weapons cache. Over the years, it had built to quite an impressive collection: pistols, rifles, and a compelling set of death-wielding knives.

There was also enough gunpowder to give his mother nightmares if she ever discovered what her third-eldest son had hidden in the space above her sitting room.

He really ought to have stored all of it at the RR Coaching Company offices in Gracechurch Street rather than here. If the explosives did go up, the family home would be reduced to rubble.

But despite his better judgement, Gus had continued to bring his ill-gotten arsenal home with him.

Home.

What were the chances he would ever see this place again?

The eve of battle always gave a man reason to consider his life choices. To question exactly the point where he had gone wrong. Only a fool willingly took up arms and went to start a war.

Augustus Trajan Jones had arrived at so many of these crossroads in his nine and twenty years that it was nigh on impossible for him to decipher which of the paths taken had led him to where he now stood.

What was clear, however, was his duty to help Armand and Evangeline La Roche. To do all he could to save them both from a senseless death.

As he leaned over and picked up a single-barrelled H.W. Mortimer shotgun from the floor, Evangeline's letter crinkled in his jacket pocket. It was a letter he had read many times.

Dear Augustus,

If you are reading this letter, then you are not dead.

Things have gone from bad to worse since you left.

My uncle has gathered a large store of weapons at the château. He means to go to war with the Lamballe gang and will not listen to me.

Please do not return to Saint-Brieuc—it is no longer safe.

Evangeline

He knew exactly why he was still carrying it weeks after it had arrived, long after he had memorized its contents. The missive had come from her.

The relationship between him and Evangeline was complicated. It always had been. But a near-death experience could give a man reason to reassess his priorities.

If Armand La Roche was determined to go to war against a rival smuggling gang in France, then Gus most certainly would be standing alongside him when the first volley was fired. He wasn't deterred by Evangeline's express command that he shouldn't come.

If she hadn't wanted me to travel to Saint-Brieuc, she wouldn't have written.

He tested the gun sights then set the rifle aside. Every piece of weaponry laid out before him had been oiled, polished, and checked.

It took some effort, but he struggled to his feet, wincing as his slowly healing chest wound protested.

Will this thing ever fully heal?

It had been six pain-filled weeks since his fellow rogue of

the road, Sir Stephen Moore, had carried the badly injured Gus on board the *Night Wind*.

There were times he woke in the dark soaked in nightmare-induced sweat. He could only pray that eventually the memory of being held down while Captain Grey dug into his flesh with a heated blade would fade. They had saved his life, but the sound of his own screams still echoed in his head.

He rubbed at the wound. A dose of laudanum would be most welcome, but Gus didn't like the way the drug addled his brain. Pain kept a man's mind sharp. It reminded him of the cost of poor decisions.

Lifting his left arm, he raised it as high as the injury would allow. The bullet fired by one of the members of Vincent Marec's gang had gone deep into the upper section of his chest, chipping off a piece of his clavicle.

There was every chance he would never again have the full use of his arm.

If I survive this next trip, I am likely going to have to retire the boat—find another way to make a living.

Over the past year or so, other members of the rogues of the road—Harry, George, and more recently, Stephen—had made the monumental decision to step away from a life of illicit dealings. All three of them were working at honest careers and had taken on wives. Only Gus and Monsale now remained embedded in their criminal endeavors, both still bachelors.

Monsale wouldn't ever change his life for a woman.

But could I?

He wasn't as set against marriage as his friend Stephen had once been, but it would take a rare lady to consider throwing her lot in with a smuggler. To know that every time her husband sailed from Portsmouth, he may not return. Finding a wife like that was proving to be a tall ask.

Gus was still staring at the weapons cache, unsure as to how much of the gunpowder he should take, when the partly ajar door swung fully open.

His father retired naval captain, William Jones, stepped into the room. He huffed and quickly closed the door behind him. Captain Jones pointed at the key in the lock. "You really should keep that turned. If any of the household servants stumble across this lot, they will surely run and tell your mother. And then there will be no living with her."

Gus scowled. He couldn't ever have the door closed, let alone locked. The attic was small; and he didn't have a good relationship with enclosed spaces.

"You know I can't do that, sir," he replied.

His father hummed his obvious disapproval. "Augustus, you are a grown man. Only children are frightened of such things."

Gus did his best to ignore the comment, having lost count of the number of times he and his father had argued over his irrational fear. It had been his main reason for not following his father into the navy. The idea of being stuck below deck with a hundred other bodies filled him with dread.

"Have you come to see me with a purpose in mind?".

His father's gaze roamed over the various weapons and crates of ammunition. "So, you are still determined to go to France? Damn. I was hoping you might change your mind."

Gus could well understand his sire's predicament. If he didn't make it back to England alive, Captain Jones was going to be left with a lot of explaining to do.

Father and son had a private understanding of what Gus had been up to both during the war and subsequent years. And while the captain had made his thoughts on the topic of smuggling quite clear, he was not about to turn his son over to the authorities.

"I have to go. They need me. The Lamballe gang are not just some local fisherman's collective who have decided they want a cut of the smuggling trade. From what Armand and Evangeline have told me, Marec is a skilled former French army officer. He knows how to lead."

His father glanced at Gus's damaged shoulder. "And his men are crack shots with a rifle."

Gus's hopes for hiding at the Duke of Monsale's residence and keeping his injury secret from his family had not lasted long. Captain Jones had been on the doorstep of Monsale House within a day of the badly wounded Gus returning to London. News of his arrival into Portsmouth Harbor had passed quickly through the network of retired naval officers and all the way to his sire.

His father laid a hand on his good shoulder. "Who else is going with you?"

Blast. I was hoping to avoid that question.

He steeled himself. "No one. Just the crew. Harry's wife is due to give birth any day. Stephen's blushing bride gave up her wedding night when he came with me last time, so I would not dare ask him again. And George swore a vow to Jane that his days of dirty deeds were behind him. They have all officially retired from the business of being rogues."

"And Monsale?"

Gus reluctantly met his father's gaze.

"You know full well he will not dare set foot in France. And I wouldn't ever ask it of him. This is my quest; and I shall not have the arrest and execution of a friend on my conscience," replied Gus.

Captain Jones pulled his son into his embrace. "And I don't suppose threatening to tell your mother the truth of the things you have been up to all these years would do me any good either?"

Gus closed his eyes and let his father's words wash over him. Lying to his mother had never sat well with him but having her know the truth would be far worse. He would much prefer that she continued to think him an honest sailor.

"No, it wouldn't." He accepted a second hug then drew back. "I had better finish up here and then go make arrangements to have the weapons I am taking to France collected.

The rest of the RR Coaching Company want to have a directors' meeting early tomorrow before I leave, so I won't have time in the morning."

"Alright, but could you at least promise me one thing?"

He forced himself to meet his father's eyes. "Name it."

"If there comes a point where you have the choice between being a bloody hero or setting aside your pride and living another day, please think of your mother. She doesn't deserve to spend the rest of her days grieving over you. And neither do I, for that matter."

Gus swallowed the lump in his throat. He couldn't blame his father for using guilt to try to make him stay. He would have done exactly the same. "You drive a hard bargain, sir, but yes. I promise not to throw my life away too cheaply. I shall keep myself constrained when it comes to heroics."

He had no intention of ever letting Vincent Marec and his men win. As far as he was concerned, the Lamballe gang would still be counting the cost of having attacked both the château and his crew long after he had finished with them. Revenge was going to be swift and complete.

His mission to France was twofold: save Evangeline and Armand, while settling a deadly score.

READ
The Rogue and the Jewel

Join my VIP readers and claim your FREE BOOK
A Wild English Rose

Also by Sasha Cottman

SERIES

The Kembal Family
The Duke of Strathmore
The Noble Lords
Rogues of the Road
London Lords

The Kembal Family

Tempted by the English Marquis
The Vagabond Viscount
The Duke of Spice

The Duke of Strathmore

Letter from a Rake
An Unsuitable Match
The Duke's Daughter
A Scottish Duke for Christmas
My Gentleman Spy
Lord of Mischief
The Ice Queen
Two of a Kind
A Lady's Heart Deceived
All is Fair in Love

Duke of Strathmore Novellas

Mistletoe and Kisses

Christmas with the Duke

A Wild English Rose

The Noble Lords

Love Lessons for the Viscount

A Lord with Wicked Intentions

A Scandalous Rogue for Lady Eliza

Unexpected Duke

The Noble Lords Boxed Set

Rogues of the Road

Rogue for Hire

Stolen by the Rogue

When a Rogue Falls

The Rogue and the Jewel

King of Rogues

The Rogues of the Road Boxed Set

London Lords

Devoted to the Spanish Duke

Promised to the Swedish Prince

Seduced by the Italian Count

Wedded to the Welsh Baron

Bound to the Belgian Count

USA Today bestselling author Sasha Cottman's novels are set around the Regency period in England, Scotland, and Europe. Her books are centred on the themes of love, honor, and family.

www.sashacottman.com

Facebook
Instagram
TikTok
Join my VIP readers and claim your FREE BOOK
A Wild English Rose

Writing as Jessica Gregory

Jessica Gregory
SASSY STEAMY ROMANCE

Jessica Gregory writes sassy steamy rom coms. She loves strong heroines and making her heroes grovel.

Royal Resorts

Room for Improvement

A Suite Temptation

The Last Resort

Sign up for Planet Billionaire and receive your FREE BOOK.

An Italian Villa Escape

Printed by Amazon Italia Logistica S.r.l.
Torrazza Piemonte (TO), Italy